Tales of
Nicolas Flamel,
Time Traveler

Ravenous Press
Berkeley, California

*Dedicated to those whose vision
encompasses all possible worlds.*

Comment by Michael Banister

While in Paris in 2011, I visited a museum located in the former home of famed alchemist Nicolas Flamel in the Marais District. Picking up a one-page flyer about the house and Flamel, I saw a reference to a book written in Portuguese, "Um Tempo Longe do Tempo," which Flamel claimed to have written. I had studied Portuguese, Spanish and French in college, and found the book title intriguing: "A Time Away from Time." I was puzzled why Flamel would have written the book in Portuguese and not French.

The blurb described the book as a memoir of Flamel's adventures in West Africa and the Caribbean in the 15th century. When I asked about getting a copy of the book, I was told that the only copy in existence was in the Rare Book Room in a library in Lisbon. When the museum guide saw how curious I was, he pointed to a bookshelf containing books about Flamel's life. I picked up one that was in French and was an autobiography. "Comment j'ai voyagé dans le temps et vécu pour raconter cette histoire (je n'ai pas encore fini)."

I asked, "Is there an English version of this?" The guide said, "No, I guess there has never been sufficient interest to justify a translation." I noticed there was no publication date on the verso of the book and asked about that. The guide had no idea when it was written.

I bought a copy with the intention of contacting the publisher or whoever had the rights. I thought I might take a crack at translating it myself.

I have to admit it was a struggle. But I did it! Ladies and gentlemen, I present to you Nicolas Flamel's own incredible story, originally written who knows when. And who knows where and when this character might show up again?

CHAPTER ONE

I suppose the first thing a person would say when picking up my autobiography is "Who is Nicolas Flamel? Never heard of him."

That's a fair question. And to answer it fairly, I'm obligated to give you a few hints. First hint—Don't assume that I am related to anyone else with the surname "Flamel"—I made up the name as a reference to an alchemical process, which I will describe later.

Second hint—you may have heard about the maritime navigation device called a "spherical astrolabe." Well, what you have never heard of is a time traveling navigation device with that name.

If you want to know more about that astrolabe and time travel, just keep reading. I'm your man!

Paris and beyond!

I was Born in 1330 in Pontoise, a village near Paris. Pontoise was the historical capital of the Gaul region of France dating from pre-Roman times. My family moved to Paris when I was 10. We were somewhat well off. My father was a bookseller specializing in rare (and expensive) books and manuscripts. My mother was a scribe whose clients were primarily wealthy people who needed to file important documents with government agencies.

My father, Josue Abreu, was a Portuguese Jew whose family had moved to West Africa to get away from the antisemitism in Portugal, and then moved to Paris. My mother, Chava Lazer, was a Jew whose family escaped to France from Russia for the same reason. I grew up with no religion, unless you consider the practice of alchemy a religion. Interestingly, it was my father's profession as a collector and seller of rare manuscripts that probably saved my life and guided my own career. Soon after our family moved to Paris when I was 10, I started suffering from muscle weakness, pain and twitching. I had trouble walking; my balance was terrible. My parents were devastated, and I was completely terrified at what had happened to my body. My father believed he had read something in one of his medical manuscripts about a treatment or cure. According to several manuscripts, there were dietary approaches, especially a diet that consisted primarily of fish and nuts. This was controversial in Paris at the time, since most people's diets prominently of lamb, beef, fowl and pork. It wasn't hard for my parents to eliminate pork, since they were Jewish. But to eliminate the other meats was nothing less than scandalous.

The new diet was miraculous! In less than 6 months I was cured. And I must say I didn't miss eating meat and came to love fish of all kinds.

As expected, I ended up following the careers of my parents. I was a moderately successful scribe. But what ultimately made me rich was buying and selling rare manuscripts. At an early age I became fascinated with some of the manuscripts my father had acquired, especially those dealing with alchemy and those describing early attempts to make a clock, a machine to tell time. Both my parents were accomplished linguists and passed that talent on to me.

Once I had established my own business as an antiquarian bookseller, I found that people were very interested in the subject of clocks, and many of my customers asked me to write something about them. At that time, only the Church's towers in big cities had what those Priests called clocks. In my research into the mechanics and history of time-keeping devices, I purchased several. Then, almost by accident (or fate?), I managed to acquire a maritime navigation device called the astrolabe that was used by sailors to determine their location by referring to the stars.

My career up to that point, although lucrative, soon took a momentous turn. I met a remarkable woman in 1360 when I was barely 30 years old. She was 10 years my senior, a wealthy benefactress named Perenelle Alarie whose family had moved to Paris from Alsace. She became one of my regular customers and shared with me a love of alchemy and ancient manuscripts. Being fluent in German as well as French, she had no difficulty translating the more esoteric manuscripts. Perenelle was taller than me and thin. She was fluent in German, French, Spanish, English and Hebrew. She shared my fascination with astrolabes and alchemy.

After 8 years of seeing Perenelle as a customer and confidant, I asked her to marry me. She agreed and we were married in 1368. We shared a phenomenal career during the next 30 years and assembled an impressive library of alchemical treatises. We also managed to succeed in several of our more controversial endeavors.

One of those endeavors was the transmutation of metals. We managed to transmute copper into a very soft form of gold. But we realized that we could not continue to do that without disastrous effects on the market value of gold! So, we agreed to destroy the results of our research and experiments.

The most controversial, but satisfying, endeavor we came upon involved modifications to a type of astrolabe—a spherical astrolabe. Here is how we learned how to perform those modifications. We encountered a phenomenal book in the year 1410. Perenelle had heard of a mysterious alchemical book from Spain. We traveled to Salamanca to see the book. It was written in Hebrew by someone named Isaac Aboab. The bookseller in Salamanca said there was a

French translation available from a bookseller in Paris. We tracked it down and bought it!

Professor Aboab's book was only 21 pages in length, was made of finely beaten lambskin, and had a cover made of copper. But the book was full of mysterious symbols and unorthodox expressions in the French translation. At times we despaired of ever completing a translation that made any sense. But in 1418, after eight years, Perenelle and I succeeded in translating it!

I am aware that the history books state that Perenelle died in 1397. Not true! Such calumnies came about probably because she was criticized, as I was, as a dabbler in "black magic." Nonsense! She was my partner in our "disappearances" into the future and past with the astrolabe. I will describe those trips in more detail in a moment; be patient! After several such voyages through time, we arranged for our last disappearances to be explained as our deaths. She and I had decided that my young assistant, Gabriel Hugo, would arrange a private "burial." I shall describe that "last" voyage with my astrolabe after I describe those preceding it.

The manuscript by Isaac Aboab was without a doubt the one that fascinated me more than all the other alchemical manuscripts we had acquired. This Professor Aboab claimed to have discovered how to convert a spherical astrolabe into a time machine!

I suppose you will be disappointed to read that I have no intention of divulging those instructions. After all, we simply cannot have two machines traveling through the interstices of time! Be content, and be assured that I have done no harm in my travels. Just the opposite, as you will soon learn!

CHAPTER TWO

A Brief Trip Here, a Brief Trip There

I I do not claim that creating our time machine was easy. On the contrary, Perenelle and I struggled with that creation for two years before we managed to get it to work. During those years, our energy often flagged and we rested by visiting museums.

The first time we actually used our astrolabe to send us on a trip through time was when Perenelle suggested that we visit the treasury of the emperor Charlemagne in the 11th century. Her reasoning was persuasive: "As you know, he was famous for his purchases of rare gems and jewelry from the Holy Land. Some of those things were reputed to have quite 'magical' properties, although they are not described." I was intrigued and we agreed to calibrate our astrolabe for the year 1046 and the treasury room of Charlemagne's palace. We had seen the palace in our own time but had never gone inside. Seeing the palace 400 years earlier would certainly be different! And not likely to be full of visitors. We hoped we would be able to directly enter the palace's treasure room without encountering anyone.

When we were ready, I placed the astrolabe on the table. We had already rehearsed the necessary procedure for activating the astrolabe. I said, "Okay, Perenelle, you place your left hand in my right hand.

Then I shall place the palm of my left hand on the bottom of the silver arrow as it extends below the astrolabe. Then, when I give you the signal, you must place the palm of your right hand on the tip of the silver arrow." I took a deep breath and asked, "Are you ready for the journey?"

"Of course, Nicolas. As I said, I have always wanted to pay a visit to Charlemagne's treasury."

She was clearly determined. So, I said, "Okay, be prepared to be surprised!"

When we touched our hands together and to the astrolabe, the room seemed to dissolve. In a few seconds, we found ourselves in Charlemagne's castle, but not exactly where we had hoped to be. It was some kind of workshop, apparently for repairs of the various collections. It seemed to be in the middle of the night and there didn't seem to be anyone around, just displays of various treasures the emperor had acquired from the Holy Land.

Perenelle immediately spotted a display table covered by lockets and necklaces from Palestine. Two items in particular caught her attention, and she picked them up. She looked at me, smiled, and said, "Nicolas, I think we should take these with us." She paused, then continued with a smile, "to study them, of course." Each of them was an oval-shaped silver amulet encrusted with rare gems. In the middle of each was a large clear gem with what looked like a strand of hair embedded within. The description on the display table said each amulet contained a hair from the Virgin Mary. The amulets were attached to long silver necklaces.

Perenelle placed one amulet over my head and the other over her own head. Then she stepped back and looked at our reflections in the tall mirror leaning against the wall. "Nicolas, they suit us perfectly," she said with a chuckle.

I said to her, "We must leave this room immediately. I am afraid we will be seen and arrested." She didn't argue, and we returned to our home and time.

Perenelle chose not to accompany me on the next foray using the astrolabe. I decided my next voyage would be to the future, and I would wear my amulet. I chose March 21, 1418, the Spring Equinox. My young apprentice, 10-year-old Gabriel Hugo, helped me at every step. Finally, I was ready to depart to the future. I remember his astonishment when I told him of my destination. "I shall not go far, only 10 years into the future. I must learn how much longer France will be ruled by the hated English."

After I announced my destination, I calibrated the astrolabe for Paris and the year 1431. I chose May 30 as the day primarily because I hoped for sunny weather, not knowing what effect rain might have on my beloved machine.

As soon as I placed both hands on the ends of the silver arrow that we had installed in the astrolabe, the room began to dissolve. The view out my window became flat. When the view became clear once again, I put the astrolabe inside my bag, put on my coat, and walked out into the glorious sunshine of the Marais District.

The scene that greeted me was terrifying. People were running here and there, chased by soldiers. I witnessed several executions of armed civilians by English soldiers. I stepped into the doorway of a shop and asked the owner what was occurring. He looked at me as if I was an imbecile and said, "The English have executed Jeanne d'Arc! Our savior!"

I replied that I had never heard of her and asked for more information. His reply astonished me. "She led our loyal French forces to victory against the English. But they captured her and have burned her at the stake!"

That was enough drama for me. Not wishing to risk my life walking around in that chaos, I made a dash back to my home, placed my hands on the ends of my astrolabe's silver arrow, and returned to the year of 1418. Young Gabriel was nowhere to be seen. Perenelle said he had been frightened by my disappearance and fled.

I was beside myself with anger at the continuation of England's aggression upon France. I told Perenelle I wanted to try one more foray into the future to see if France would soon become independent of the hated English. I chose a random date, December of 1453. With the amulet around my neck, I set the astrolabe on the table, set the date, and again set the location as Paris. Placing my hands on the ends of the silver arrow, I once again saw the scene outside my window blur, waver, and become clear. I put the astrolabe inside my bag and prepared for the worst—or the best!

This time, as I walked outside onto the street, the scene was very different. People were jubilant, dancing in the streets and cheering the capture of Bordeaux by the forces of French King Charles VII. I asked a passerby whether this victory was part of the long war between England and France that had begun in 1337. The answer was a resounding and joyful "Yes!"

Not having brought with me much money, clothing or anything that could have sustained me for any length of time, I wisely decided to walk back to my house and return to my own time. As I walked, I purchased a newspaper from an urchin standing on the corner. I hope I can learn more about these events!

CHAPTER THREE

Leaving Paris (Almost) for Good!

I still remember the shock I experienced as I read that newspaper. In addition to the political and social news, there were two notices for the sale of African slaves from Mali! I looked again at the date on the newspaper—1453. I had no idea how slavery could have been introduced into France. But when I closely read the two notices, I saw that the company selling the slaves was a Portuguese company doing business in France and Spain. The company claimed to be under the sponsorship of a Portuguese duke that had begun taking Africans seven years before, in 1446, from the village of Jenne, on the Gambia River in West Africa.

Probably as a result of reading that newspaper, I thought I might make a trip to that village in the year 1446 to see how this slave trading came to be.

That night I had a very strange dream. My dream that night was… what? A revelation? I suppose it was. Because here is what happened in that dream. I was walking along a road in Spain talking to Abraham Zacuto. Even though I hadn't met the man in real life, I had heard of him. He was a Jewish mystic, the royal astronomer for the Portuguese King John II. As Zacuto and I walked, he told me of

9

his own version of a spherical astrolabe! His story was so shocking that it almost woke me up. Then something even more shocking happened in the dream. Zacuto looked at me with his piercing gaze and said, "Nicolas Abreu, you have a task to complete. Another voyage through time." He stopped as we approached a tremendous oak at the side of the road. "Let us sit in the shade while I describe your task."

We made ourselves comfortable, and Zacuto resumed his story. "You are right to be outraged about the advent of slavery in our world. It must be stopped! Before it continues it must be stopped!" I was about to ask how it began when he read my mind. "It was the Portuguese who commenced this unholy enslavement of human beings from Africa." At this point, Zacuto looked at me and said, "Now, what I am about to tell you will confuse you. But be assured it is the truth and will become clear.

"First, you and Perenelle must make another astrolabe like yours. Except—and this is very important! Once the new astrolabe is functional, you must carefully break the silver wire that passes through the golden globe inside the astrolabe. Then you will take it with you as you calibrate your original spherical astrolabe to a time in the distant future, the year 2018. You will also calibrate the location to a village on an island nation in the Pacific Ocean called Hawaii. And be sure you are each wearing your amulets; they are capable of absorbing some of the power of the astrolabe.

"When you and Perenelle place your hands on the ends of the silver arrow passing through your astrolabe, you will be transported through time and space to a rustic Hawaiian village called Kalaupapa, where you will see an unoccupied derelict mansion.

"Enter the mansion through the unlocked back door. There will be several attics. Place a ladder underneath the middle attic and enter it. Inside you will find a large trunk. Inside that trunk will be a small chest. The chest will be empty. Nearby you will see a small bookshelf full of books."

Now, Zacuto paused to catch his breath. He resumed and once again stared at me. "Nicolas, what I will tell you now will be difficult to understand, but trust me. You must wrap the broken astrolabe you just created in a blanket, place it inside the small chest, and place a few books on top of the blanket. Then you must put the chest back into the trunk and close it.

"At that point, history itself will change. By placing the broken astrolabe there, our path through history will cross another path, and that path will become our path. That small chest? On the new path, the chest will not only contain your astrolabe and the few random books you had placed inside. Now it will also contain a strange new book! A memoir of a man named Horacio Fuente describing his remarkable journey to the African city of Mogadishu and his new life there.

"But there is more! Listen carefully. In this new path, you will recall a visit you made to the West African village of Jenne. Yes, you made that trip in your new past, and you will now recall it!

At this point, I interrupted Zacuto. "But Master, how will what I do cause history to change? How will a book suddenly appear inside the chest, where no book was there before? How will I recall a place I've never been to?"

Zacuto again seemed short of breath. After a long pause, he resumed his explanation. "A new historical pathway will cross the interstice between possible histories and replace the current history. It will be as if the world itself had changed. The new history will unfold in unforeseen ways. That is the only way I know how to describe the process.

"The book that appears in the chest will recount what had occurred in the past of that new history. It will describe how the astrolabe was modified but not who modified it. The book will contain detailed instructions on how to repair the astrolabe to render it functional as a time machine."

Once again, I interrupted. "But I don't understand. Where did this

Horacio Fuente come from? How did he come across the astrolabe? What was he doing in East Africa?" I was becoming frustrated, but I was also worried that my dream would end before Master Zacuto provided answers to my questions.

"Nicolas, after you leave this dream you will travel to the date of November 1, 2018, and perform the task I described. You will then remember your new past and embark on more travels to the future.

"After you return from 2018, the next destination you must travel to will be the one you already have in mind—the year 1446 and the location is the city of Niumi, in Mali, West Africa. As I have explained, you will recall having spent time in Mali in your new past, in a village called Jenne.

"Once you arrive in Niumi, proceed to the grand mosque and ask to speak with a local nobleman named Duke Gbèré Keita, known as the 'Mansa.' You will be escorted to his office, where you will await the arrival of three sisters from near-future Gambia. They will explain to the Mansa how they arrived and what their mission is. At that point, you will understand what transpired. The sisters will recognize you from the time you were in Jenne. That seems incomprehensible to you now, but you will comprehend it at that time. Good luck and God Speed!"

CHAPTER FOUR

The Strange World of the Future!

O nce my dream ended—or I should say once Master Zacuto departed my dream—I had trouble waking up. Perhaps it was worry that prevented me from fully awakening. Worry about what I should do next. How to do what I should do next. What would happen in my next voyage, to my next destination. When I got up, I noticed that Perenelle was already awake, and she was watching me. She said she knew I had been dreaming because she was awakened by me talking in my sleep. I explained what had occurred in my dream. She was astounded at what I described to her. But then she decided she wanted to accompany me on those voyages to the future, at least to Hawaii but perhaps not Mali. "Nicolas, you may need my help. And besides that, I am more than curious about that strange story. When shall we go?"

I could tell she was serious, and I knew she would be good company, not to mention an able partner should complications occur. "As I explained, in my dream, Master Zacuto instructed me to make a second astrolabe like the one we already have. That's so we can leave it in the attic of the mansion in Hawaii." Perenelle agreed, and for the next several days we devoted ourselves to making a second astrolabe.

Because we had already modified one astrolabe and still had extra materials—silver wire, emerald-green chrome tourmaline gemstones, and pieces of platinum—converting our second one into a time-traveling spherical astrolabe was not difficult. But before connecting that new astrolabe's silver wire to both ends of the arrow, I left one end disconnected, as if it had been broken, as instructed by Master Zacuto.

Perenelle put the new, broken, astrolabe in the backpack and hoisted it onto my back. We placed our amulets around our necks. Then we stood next to the table where the original astrolabe was sitting. I had adjusted the date band for October 1, 2018, and the location for Kalaupapa, Hawaii. When we were ready, we placed our hands on the astrolabe as we had done before. She placed her left hand in my right hand, I placed the palm of my left hand on the bottom of the silver arrow. Then I looked at Perenelle, smiled, and said, "On my count of three, place your palm on the arrow's tip."

On my count of three, she touched the arrow. Immediately, we could feel our amulets vibrating. The room began fading away. The view out our window turned flat and wavy. In a few seconds, we were no longer in our drawing room in Paris. We were standing on a gravel road in a tropical region somewhere. Despite it being November, the weather was warm and humid. There was a slight breeze. There were fields of pineapple and guava trees on either side of the road. In the distance, I could see the ocean. I turned to see if Perenelle was okay. She was wide-eyed and smiling. "Nicolas, this surely looks like paradise!"

I looked from side to side, but saw no signs of any homes or other signs of habitation. I placed our astrolabe inside Perenelle's backpack and said, "I think we should continue walking along this road towards the ocean. My dream said the mansion we must find would be on a cliff overlooking the ocean."

We began walking along the road. Soon we heard a rumbling noise approaching from behind us. I couldn't imagine what it was, so I said, "Quick, let us get off this road and hide for a bit. The noise might be a cart or a wagon of some type, but the noise is becoming a roar!"

As we crouched behind a cluster of tall bushes, we saw something we had never seen before. It was a cart made of metal, completely enclosed with windows on all sides. The cart's wheels appeared to be made of rubber. There was a woman inside the cart with her hands on what appeared to be some type of steering wheel. A foul-smelling smoke came out of a pipe extending from the rear of the cart. We watched as the cart pulled over to the side of the road. It became silent and the smoke stopped coming out of the pipe at the rear. The woman opened her door, stepped out of the cart and waved to us.

Perenelle waved back and spoke to her in French. The woman looked puzzled and shook her head. Then Perenelle said something in English. "Hello. We are lost. We are looking for a mansion nearby. We heard it was for sale. Is it at the end of this road?"

The woman smiled and nodded. "Yes. If you keep walking in the direction you're headed, you'll come to it in a few minutes. By the way, the owner of the mansion you're interested in is a very reclusive man from China. The mansion hasn't been lived in for a few years, but I hear it's in pretty good shape. The real estate agent who listed the property has an office in town, back the way you came. I hope you like the property, we could use a few more inhabitants around here. Good luck!"

I smiled and replied, "Thank you very much. I do hope we find it to our liking."

The woman started to get back in her vehicle but then turned and said, "By the way, after you have a look at the mansion, stop by my office and I can tell you how to contact the real estate agent." She reached into her breast pocket, pulled out a card and handed it to Perenelle, saying "Here's my business card with the address of my office." Then she got back in her vehicle, turned on the motor and drove away. After a short distance, we saw her turn left onto another road. Perenelle and I kept walking, hoping to see our destination soon.

It wasn't long before Perenelle said she could see the mansion in the distance. Soon, we walked onto the grounds. "It's magnificent! I wish, Nicolas, that you and I could purchase it."

I smiled and said, "Yes, I certainly wouldn't mind embarking on a new adventure here on this island. But as you know, we have work to do." We turned and walked around the left side of the building and approached the rear door. Finding it open, we entered and stood agape at the sheer beauty of that building. Then we walked through the parlor and walked up the stairs to the left. We turned right and walked up another set of stairs. Finally, it seemed we were on the top floor. We could see there were three attic doors on the ceiling. Choosing the center one, I placed a ladder underneath it. I turned to Perenelle and said, "Shall I go up first?" She nodded and reached out to take hold of the ladder to steady it. I began climbing.

When I reached the top, I pushed open the attic door and moved it aside. Then I hoisted myself up and inside the attic. I turned back and said, "Okay, Perenelle. I will hold the top of the ladder steady as you climb up."

Once she was in the attic, we crawled over to the trunk, opened it and removed the small chest. It was empty. Following Zacuto's instructions, we carefully placed the broken astrolabe inside, covered it with books from a nearby pile, and closed the chest. Then we lifted the chest and placed it back inside the trunk. That task completed, we climbed back down the ladder to the main floor and stood waiting.

Perenelle said, "Did you feel that? A sort of vibration? Nicolas, you look dazed. Are you okay? Do you need to sit down?"

I felt like I would faint unless I sat down. I remembered Zacuto's prediction. Then I said, "Perenelle, he was right. I now remember visiting the Malian city of Jenne, even though I have never been there! At least… not in my former world. That's it—we have crossed over the interstice between the worlds, Perenelle! And I remember meeting and talking to the three time-traveling sisters from their future!"

Perenelle looked shocked. Then she said, "I think you're right. As I said, it did feel like something vibrated briefly. But I do not remember meeting anyone in that village, or in Mali for that matter! My memories seem to be suffused with where we are now—this island paradise of Hawaii! I wonder why that would be."

I added, "And I felt a powerful vibration from my amulet. Did you feel the same from yours?"

"Yes, now that you mention it. Do you suppose our amulets have absorbed some of the power of the astrolabe?"

I paused, then said, "I suppose this is the beginning. Onto our next destination—Mali!"

After we had walked back outside, Perenelle put her hand on my shoulder and said, "I can't wait to see this new world! But… Nicolas, I have a strong recollection that I will not accompany you on that particular journey. My memory tells me that you and I will meet in another time in the future, in a different place. Perhaps somewhere in Hawaii!"

CHAPTER FIVE

Going our Separate Ways

After we had walked out to the back of the mansion, we placed our astrolabe on a table. But before I could calibrate it for our return to our home and time, Perenelle stopped me again. "Nicolas, I shall remain here, in paradise. As I said, my new memory tells me that I have things to do here. And that you and I shall meet back here in the future."

I was shocked. For a moment, I stood still and looked out at the view of the ocean in the blue distance. Then I seemed to come to and said, "Perenelle, my darling. I am surprised, but somehow, I understand. I accept your wisdom in this. We each have our amulets, so we can travel through time with them. I shall take the astrolabe with me and use it as necessary."

Perenelle stood by as I placed my hands together and on the tips of the silver arrow. I then saw the view waver for a few seconds and then change.

I was back in my dining room. Perenelle was gone; she had not accompanied me. I was full of anxiety—would I ever see her again?

I didn't tarry there in our home. It was time to choose my next destination. This time the destination was Niumi, Mali, West Africa, in the year 1446. I set the date and location bands accordingly.

Not just Mali; that was strange enough. But a big city in Mali—Niumi, which I had never heard of. Before I could stop myself, I burst out laughing. But then I muttered to myself, "I know what you're thinking, Nicolas. You're laughing because you gave no thought to picking out a wardrobe for such an excursion!! Is the city tropical? Savannah? Pretty like Paris?"

I wondered what kind of people I would meet. I had met a few Africans in Europe, but admittedly I knew nothing about them. I found them exotic with their bold clothes and black skin. But I also knew some that seemed more Arab than African. Even some with blue eyes! Especially the Moroccans from Spain. I hoped some of the Malians I would meet could speak French!

Then I said aloud, "Well, let's get this over with." In my dream, Master Zacuto had told me that everything would become clear once I arrived in Niumi. I hoped that would be true.

Then I realized I would have to bring some type of money that might be acceptable in Africa. Silver and gold coins would definitely be acceptable. I went into our study and retrieved a large pouch of gold and silver coins Perenelle and I had collected over the years. I put some coins in my pockets and felt ready to depart.

Niumi, Mali

As before, I placed one of my hands on the tip of the silver arrow. Then I placed the palm of my other hand on the bottom of the arrow. The view wavered for a few seconds, then the scene in front of me changed.

Instead of the view of the ocean, I now saw a view of a wide river with a vast jungle beyond. There were flat-bottomed boats on the river being poled by African people. Some of the boats were piled high with goods of some sort. Other boats were full of passengers. Many of them wore what looked like Muslim clothing—men wearing some type of turban, women wearing scarves and long dresses.

I was standing on a dirt road near a group of buildings that fronted the river. Boats were tied up in front of one of the buildings. I mumbled, "This might be some sort of boat rental place. I should find someone who can tell me where I am."

I was breathless and very excited. I realized I would first need to purchase some clothing more typical of a Muslim man rather than a Parisian man. I walked toward an area full of shops and found one that sold clothing. I was relieved to find that my French was readily understood. The proprietor assisted me in putting on one of those wrap-around cloaks I had seen Arab men wearing in Paris.

I walked out of the shop and headed toward a large town I could see in the distance. Soon I came upon a grand, beautiful mosque. Again, as Master Zacuto had told me, I seemed to recognize the mosque. And I had a premonition that I would know what to do after I entered the mosque's office to the side of the sanctuary.

I walked up to the entrance of the office and was greeted by a guard. He introduced himself as Arash and told me to follow him inside. A richly dressed African man sat on a beautiful Persian carpet in the middle of the room. Arash said, "Duke Keita, Master Flamel has arrived as expected." I should have been shocked, but instead that feeling of déjà vu supplanted my surprise.

I knew then the purpose of my visit. I approached Keita, bowed and said, "My Lord, you will soon have visitors. Three young women from the village of Jenne. They will present to you a most remarkable proposal."

Keita nodded and gestured for me to sit beside him. He bade me tell him more about the visitors. "Their names are Khadijah, Maryam and Sofia. They are sisters."

"And their purpose in seeking an audience with me?"

"They propose an expedition to the nearby islands in the Great Ocean. An expedition composed of several of your large, sail-equipped pirogues."

"Why should I be interested in such an expedition?"

"Your Excellency, your kingdom will soon be visited by Portuguese explorers. At first, they will seem to be innocent traders interested in establishing a business relationship involving goods from Europe and goods from Mali. But that professed interest masks their actual interest—purchasing people rather than goods. They seek to export slaves to Europe in order to improve their economy and make it more competitive with the economy of Spain and England."

"Slaves? That is outrageous! I would never sell my own people into slavery."

"Yes, I understand and I quite agree with you. But these Portuguese anticipate your reaction to their proposal, and are prepared to take your people into slavery by force."

"But how do you know this, Master Flamel? You are French. Do you know these Portuguese?"

At this point, I realized how awkward it would be for the duke to comprehend, let alone believe, the story I would tell him. "Yes, I am French. And it was in my home city of Paris that I first learned of the Portuguese plans to introduce slavery in Portugal. But, Sire, I think you should hear the story of slavery from the sisters themselves. I believe their arrival is imminent."

Keita sat quietly for a few moments. He seemed to be considering what I had just told him. Then he looked at me and said, "Flamel, I will listen to these sisters' presentation. You say they have a plan. I will listen and consider it."

I didn't have to wait long for the sisters to appear. They seemed surprised to see me there. I was surprised as well when one of them, I believe it was Khadijah, said she thought she recognized me but didn't recall ever having met me. I then had one of those "new" memories that sprang forth. I told her she probably remembered seeing me in her village of Jenne, where I had visited years earlier. Honestly, I cannot fathom how I could have remembered such a thing, let alone ever having been in Jenne. I must assume that Master

Zacuto was speaking truthfully when he told me in my dream that once Perenelle and I had placed the astrolabe in the attic chest it would give rise to new "memories" of a life in what he called a "parallel" world.

The meeting of the sisters and the duke progressed as I somehow knew it would. They presented their proposal for a fleet of large pirogues that would transport Malians and goods to the islands some distance west of the mainland. I was relieved to hear that Keita knew of the islands, at least through legends from several hundred years in the past. He agreed to the sisters' proposal.

I had little involvement in the next stages of that grand Malian enterprise. The sisters and Keita arranged everything—transport on river pirogues from the city to the coast, procuring large, sail-equipped pirogues, and loading the pirogues with supplies and willing volunteers who eagerly looked forward to a new adventure.

The sisters had explained to Keita that this enterprise would require a 10-year commitment to build a community on the main island of the group, an island that we know today as Santiago Island. Maryam explained the project: "In 10 years, three Portuguese caravels commanded by Antonio de Noli, Alvise Cadamosto and Diogo Gomes will drop anchor at the nearest island to your coast. Quite by accident, as it happened. Historical accounts from that time say the ships were blown off course. The island is uninhabited, as are the other nine islands in the group. The Portuguese will name the island group 'Cabo Verde.' Fortunately for our purposes, the Portuguese will drop anchor at the southern tip of a peninsula that blocks the view of a bay. The banks of the bay are heavily forested, as is most of the island. Our little colony of Malians will have confined their building efforts to the land on the far side of the bay behind the peninsula, well-hidden from view."

At this point, I knew what Keita's reaction would be, and what I would have to do to mitigate his shock. Keita expressed his shock at what Maryam had said. He raised his eyebrows and said, "So, exactly how do you know the plans of the Portuguese 10 years from now?"

I suppressed a chuckle at Sofia's reply. "I'm surprised, your esteemed advisor, Nicolas Flamel, has not explained how our journey began and from whence we came."

Keita turned to me with a questioning look on his face. I told him the truth. "They have come from the future, My Lord. I gave them a gift, albeit not personally, and in a very round-about way. Do you wish a more detailed explanation?"

Keita drummed his fingers on the table, arose, turned, and looked out the window. Then he returned to the table and said to Sofia, "You came from the future. But you are plainly Malian. You speak Fulani with a Jenne accent, as if it were your native tongue. You also speak Portuguese. I have many questions, but I will put those questions aside for the time being. But the question that burns in my mind is this—Please explain the Portuguese sailors' reaction when they encounter a little colony of Malians."

Maryam explained. "Father Rodrigo, our benefactor, the priest who came up with our plan and sent us on our journey here from 44 years in the future, created a masterful plan. Three huts will be constructed on the peninsula where the Portuguese ships will anchor to investigate the island and replenish their supplies of food and water. As the crew rows ashore in their dinghies, they will see an acre of beans beside the huts. They will see half a dozen women in that field picking beans and putting them into baskets. Once all the crew members are ashore, the women will walk toward them as if to greet them. Instead, they will take knives out of their baskets and warn them to stop. Half a dozen armed Malian soldiers will emerge from each of the huts and take the sailors prisoner. Then two heavily armed pirogues will emerge from the bay and block the sailors from returning to their caravels."

I could see that Keita was not convinced. He replied sarcastically, "I see. And after taking the sailors prisoner, we will take possession of three armed caravels with which to challenge the hegemony of the

European powers. I eagerly await your explanation of how we will learn to sail caravels, let alone enlisting the crew to teach us!"

Khadijah smiled and said, "Well, don't forget, we will have 10 years to prepare our European surprise!" She turned to Maryam and said, "My sister, why don't you remove the maps from your pack."

Maryam took her pack off, removed the maps, unrolled the map of the Cabo Verde Islands and spread it out on the table. Keita, myself and the others approached the table. Maryam asked Keita and me to hold down the ends of the map. "The map shows the group of islands to the west of the African continent." Pointing to one of the islands she said, "This island here is closest to the African coast where the Gambia River flows out into the sea. In the future whence we came, the Portuguese, when they discover the islands, will name the islands Cabo Verde. They will name this island here Santiago. That is here we should establish our greeting party for the Portuguese crews. Once we have taken them into custody, perhaps we shall put them to work clearing more land.

"We know from our study of history that the crews on those ships were Africans, taken as slaves from a previous raid on the coast. Those crews will willingly assist us in learning to sail the caravels. Then we shall put the second part of our plan into plan—sailing north to destroy the Portuguese and Spanish ship-building operations."

I could see the shock on Keita's face as he digested this information. I too should have been shocked, but as before, the foreknowledge of that plan appeared in my mind as Maryam gave her presentation. The meeting came to an end, and Keita escorted the sisters and me into a small, intimate dining room where we had a leisurely lunch. Keita said to one of the staff, "Please inform Arash to arrange for the sisters to lodge here in one of the mosque auxiliary buildings." Turning to Khadijah, he said, "Tomorrow we shall meet here again and go over the details of this grand plan you have presented."

Santiago Island

I was pleasantly surprised to see how expeditiously the sisters' plans came to fruition. For the next four years the Malians sent four fleets of massive pirogues to Santiago Island. The latest fleet arrived in 1452. It transported mostly men skilled in lumber work, women skilled in extending trails deep into the forest surrounding the bay, and men and women skilled in carpentry and iron work. Duke Keita, who had returned to the mainland the year before to make sure all was secure in his kingdom, was aboard the next fleet to the island and was eager to see what progress had been made on the "village" the Malians had made. It was his first trip back since the colony began taking shape.

Maryam and I were working on the roof of one of the new buildings when Keita approached and said, "I must say these buildings look quite a bit more substantial than the shacks you're planning to construct on the beach on the peninsula."

Maryam laughed and said, "Of course. This will eventually be a village of substantial size, stretching well back into the forest. Those 'shacks' as you call them must be built to look like primitive dwellings to the Portuguese sailors when they arrive."

Keita smiled. "Only four more years! I'll wager everyone in this colony is looking forward to that!"

Maryam looked serious. "Well, yes and no. Certainly it will be exciting, but also dangerous. We really don't know with any certainty how many crewmen will be aboard those caravels. Father Rodrigo read varying accounts of the Portuguese landing. The more reliable accounts, however, said the crews consisted of a captain and 10 to 12 sailors on each ship. We do know who the three captains will be— Antonio de Noli, Alvise Cadamosto and Diogo Gomes. Some of the crewmembers will be Africans taken as slaves earlier when the ships went up the Gambia River. Others might be indentured Portuguese working off their debts. Most of the holds will be filled with goods to be traded upriver. Of course, when the storm blows those ships west away from the coast, they will end up here."

Keita said, "Well, with this latest shipment of goods we've brought quite a large supply of weapons. The final group of pirogues will be sent here in three years, and it will be transporting several dozen soldiers. We'll be expecting the Portuguese to arrive less than two months later."

I have to confess I was more than a little nervous at the thought of how that confrontation might take place. It was a piece of information that my dream informant hadn't included. Nevertheless, I put my apprehension aside and got to work doing my part in the development of our little Cape Verde-Malian community.

For the next several years, a group of Malians and myself explored the other islands in the Cape Verde group to gauge their suitability for development. We were fortunate to see that several of the islands were just as beautiful, pristine and worthy of development as Santiago Island. We prepared an ambitious development project that we estimated would take three years.

It was upon my return to Santiago Island to report on our progress that I heard the shocking story of the Santiago Malians' confrontation with the Portuguese fleet in 1456. I heard the story directly from one of the Africans who had been a slave on Cadamosto's caravel. Youssef was his name. His account of the capture of the Portuguese ships and crew was nothing less than astounding.

I had known the general outline of the sisters' plan to trick the Portuguese into thinking the island was inhabited only by a few, simple indigenous natives. The Malians would build a few shacks and a small garden on the shore where the Portuguese ships would drop anchor, and then lure the sailors into thinking they could easily overpower the women working in the garden. Then the sisters would pull out knives and take the sailors' captains prisoner. At that point a group of armed Malians would emerge from the shacks to seize the rest of the sailors and commandeer the caravels.

According to Youssef, the plan was wildly successful, although not without an unexpected turn of events that could have turned into a disaster for the Malians. Youssef explained what happened. "The first part of the sisters' plan started out fine, with them surprising the three captains and stopping them at knifepoint. Khadijah gave an amazing order in clear Portuguese: 'In the name of His Lordship Keita of Mali, I order you to stop and raise your hands. You are under arrest for violating his sovereign territory. Your ships and their contents are forfeit!' At first, the captains and sailors complied. A moment later, half a dozen armed Malian soldiers emerged from each of the three huts and approached. Khadijah continued, 'You will be taken prisoner. You will not be harmed unless you resist. I warn you, do not resist or it will be the last thing you do!'"

Youssef paused. Then he took a breath and continued. "Instead of complying with Khadijah's order, Captain Cadamosto lunged at her, spun her around and pulled her knife out of her hand. Then he wrapped one arm around her, pinning her arms against her torso, held the knife up in the air, and said to her, 'Order everyone to drop their weapons or I'll kill you.'"

I have to confess to my alarm at hearing Youssef's account. I asked him to continue. Youssef then told me the most amazing thing. "Instead of obeying Cadamosto's command, Khadijah said nothing and stood still. Master Flamel, I am proud to say that we Africans saw an opportunity and seized it. One of my fellow African slaves on the ships, Hassan, lunged at Cadamosto from behind, wrested away the knife, and plunged it deep into his back, killing him instantly. Then Hassan threw the knife to my cousin Kareem, who used it to stab Antonio de Noli to death.

"Before anyone could react, the third Portuguese captain, Diogo Gomes, took out his own knife and started to run toward Khadijah. Maryam intercepted him and plunged her own knife deep into his chest, killing him.

"Once the three captains were lying on the ground, dead, Kareem threw down his knife. He and Hassan raised their hands to let the sisters know whose side they were on."

I was astounded at this account. I told him how fortuitous it was that the Africans had turned against their would-be masters and killed them. "Youssef, I think it fair to say the Africans saved this Malian development program and prevented the Portuguese invasion of the New World."

The next three years were memorable in several ways. First there were the continuing development projects we had undertaken on the islands, projects that I had taken an active role in. I must confess that I never thought I would become skilled at construction!

Another memorable experience, shared by all of us including me, was learning how to sail the caravels the Malians had "liberated" from the Portuguese. The Malians' plan was to use the caravels to sail back across the Great Ocean and attack the naval ports of the Portuguese and Spanish. I would not join them in that undertaking, as I had my hands full in the various development projects on the islands.

I often stood on our dock and watched as the three formerly Portuguese caravels were being prepared for departure. The sisters had decided that each of them would sail on a separate ship as Chief Mate under an experienced Gambian as Captain. Hassan would captain the "Fatouma" with Khadija as Chief Mate. Kareem would captain the "Oumou" with Sofia as Chief Mate. Youssef would captain the "Aissata" with Maryam as Chief Mate. Khalil, Adil and Salman would each be Second Mate on the ships. The three other Africans would be Mates. Each caravel would have 24 additional crew chosen from the Malian soldiers.

In November of 1459, it was decided the ships' departure would take place that month. The week before their departure had been devoted to thoroughly inspecting the ships for seaworthiness, loading the ships with cannon balls and supplies, and installing on each ship two pirogues fitted with oars for eight men. Two lightweight swivel guns had been installed on each pirogue, along with a supply of lead ball shot, a catapult and dozens of pots of flammable oil.

The Malians Attack Portugal and Spain!

At dawn on the 21st of the month, the well-armed Malian fleet sailed out of our harbor for its historic attacks on the ports of Portugal and Spain. The first leg of the fleet's voyage would take a month. The plan was to attack the Portuguese port of Lagos with firepots and cannon. The plan anticipated that because of nearness to Christmas, most or all of the Portuguese port workers and sailors would be ashore celebrating. The Malians and Gambians would destroy the docks, seize several Portuguese caravels, and sail back out to sea to prepare for a similar attack on the Spanish port of Huelga. After the attack on that port, the plan was to proceed to the island of Madeira, which was occupied by Portuguese colonists, and perform the same destructive operation. The final piece of the plan was to sail to the Canary Islands and attack the Spanish ports of La Palma, Tenerife and Gran Canaria.

I received the reports of the wildly successful attacks when our fleet returned at the end of 1460. Everything went according to plan. Our navy had captured six Portuguese and Spanish caravels and added them to our fleet. We also had liberated several African slaves who willingly joined our navy.

Over the next three years we completed our development of four of our islands, which now boasted ports, housing and factories. We adopted a plan prepared by Maryam and Youssef that would blockade the Azores Islands. Our navy would "decorate" the markings of our newly acquired caravels as those of Spain, sail them to the Azores and block the ports from being taken by the Portuguese. That would of course further inflame relations between the Spanish and Portuguese kingdoms.

The plan was a success. In the year 1466, the Malian crews successfully joined with the African slaves on the Azores and overthrew what passed as a "government." The Malians persuaded the slaves and the indentured Portuguese "colonists" to join the Malians. Those indentured Portuguese and slaves not only overthrew the overlords, they killed them.

During that same year, a few of our ships posing as Portuguese ships sailed to the Canaries and assisted the native Guanche people in overthrowing the Spanish colonizers. The Guanche, in a showing of gratitude, gave us full access to the ports built by the Spanish and handed over 4 of the 6 caravels built by the Spanish. The Guanche kept one caravel for their own use. The remaining Spanish caravel escaped our attack and sailed south. But the crew members were Guanche slaves, who it was expected would soon overthrow the Spanish officers. At that point it was time for us to recoup our strength at home and consolidate our gains.

CHAPTER SIX

The New World!

A fter another 10 years, we were ready to begin planning one of our most ambitious projects yet. By 1471 we had successfully built a fleet of caravels and recruited crews and colonists for our plan to sail west across the Great Ocean from the Cabo Verde Islands to the continent I knew would become "Brazil" in the future. I would not be joining them because, as always, I was extremely busy with the development of our islands. Of course, accomplishments always take longer than the plans. It was 10 years, 1481, before a Malian fleet of three caravels would successfully cross the Great Ocean and drop anchor in the bay off the coast of Brazil. On this voyage the "Oumou" was captained by Sofia Amina, the "Kassa" was captained by Kareem ibn Hamid, and "Aissata" was captained by Khalil ibn Yousef.

I heard about the voyage three years later, in 1484, from Captain Kareem of the "Kassa." He told me that the Malian fleet arrived in 1481 at a vast continent across the Great Ocean, a continent that would eventually become known as "Quonambec." I have a pretty good recollection of the report he gave to me after the Aissata had returned to Santiago Island to take on more supplies:

"Nicolas, we were astonished by everything we saw! The dwellings resembled those of Mali. Indeed, the first man we encountered was himself an African man named Musa ibn Jabreel. He told us that his parents, who were young children at the time, were part of an expedition sent across the Great Ocean by the great Mansa Musa more than 100 years before. Only three boats survived the crossing. The survivors built primitive buildings and docks, most of which were still standing, although in very poor shape.

"I introduced myself and our crews. When I told him about our cargo, which included building materials, he smiled and asked, 'And what do you plan on doing with your building materials? Are you lost, or is this an invasion?'

"Sofia explained to Musa that it wasn't invasion but that our arrival was not an accident. She told him that we had a proposal. Musa looked interested, but first he asked us about our ships. He had never seen such large ships. Sofia told him that they were called caravels and had been originally developed years ago by the Portuguese. She then told him about the arrival of the three Portuguese ships and the attempt to take us prisoner. She described how we defeated them, took their ships and learned to sail them with the help of the liberated African slaves aboard the ships.

"Musa said he had never heard of the Portuguese. Sofia explained where they came from and described their attempts to enslave the African people. Salman and I told Musa that we had been two of the slaves aboard the Portuguese ships.

"When Sofia told Musa that her people had managed to put a temporary end to the Portuguese slave raids, Musa asked how it was possible to do that with only the three caravels they had seized from the Portuguese. Sofia then described the Malians' attacks on the ports of Portugal and Spain in which many slaves were freed and more caravels seized and put into the service of the Malian navy.

"After that, Nicolas, other people emerged from the forest carrying gutted deer they had killed during a hunt. There were six men, three women and four adolescent boys. Nicolas, those people were amazing! The women appeared to be natives, perhaps 30 to 35 years old. Three of the men appeared to be African of the same age. Three other men were also African but appeared to be about 10 years older. The adolescent boys appeared to be of mixed African and native ancestry."

I was intrigued by what I had heard, but even more amazed at the rest of the story. Sofia and the others proposed to assist the local people develop better housing and teach them to build better ships, especially caravels. Musa and the others prepared a feast for them.

North to Guanahani

During those three years, the Malians helped the local people build several caravels for their own use, better houses, another school and a larger community dining hall. It was at the conclusion of that period that a remarkable young local woman, Iracema, was allowed to join the crew on the Aissata on its return to Santiago and then on to Mali to take on more supplies for the new land of Quonambec. After somewhat more than two months, the Aissata arrived at Santiago Island.

That was where I first met this remarkable young woman, Iracema. The very first thing she asked me was to tell her more about the "time machine" she had heard the Malians talk about as they explained how they knew the location of Quonambec. I told Iracema I had left the machine in the distant future after I discovered its power had been absorbed by an amulet that I had acquired from a Parisian emperor on one of my voyages to the distant past.

But what Iracema really wanted to talk about was her idea of outfitting a naval fleet to dispatch to the islands north of Quonambec in order to protect the indigenous people from the predations of the Spanish and Portuguese. In particular, she suggested the fleet should be composed entirely of indigenous people rather than Africans, in order to ensure the trust of the local people. I told her it would be a wonderful idea and suggested she present it to Duke Gbére Keita when she arrived in Mali.

Six years later, in 1490, I received a report from Duke Keita on his arrival back to Santiago Island. His report was more comprehensive than the message I had received earlier from Captains Iracema and Janaina on the progress of development of Guanahani Island. That development would raise the standard of living of the local people and would hopefully protect them from the predations of Cristoforo Colombo's fleet when it was expected to arrive in 1492. I'll paraphrase what Keita told me:

"The people, with instruction and assistance from the Quonambec expedition, have completed an ambitious program of building homes, shipping infrastructure, fortifications and improved farming techniques. In addition, Iracema's crews have shown the people how to build sail-equipped pirogues, using the pirogues on board the caravels as models. Iracema has recruited three crews of indigenous people, and they have begun sailing to the nearby islands to assist those people in developing and fortifying their lands. In fact, by now those projects are well underway. There is even an ongoing caravel-building project. That project required more hardwood than the island can grow, which was the purpose of Captains Iracema and Janaina's voyage to Quonambec.

"While Iracema and Janaina were in Quonambec they obtained another caravel for the return to Guanahani. They loaded their ships with hardwood lumber, iron tools and other building supplies."

At that point, Keita paused to collect his thoughts. Then he said, "Nicolas, you might recall hearing about a group of Guanche people from the Canaries who had been abducted in the past and forced to work on board a Spanish ship. Well, a month ago we received a report that the Guanches overpowered the Spanish officers, threw them overboard and surrendered the ship to a pursuing Malian Navy ship. The Malians took the Guanches back to the Canaries, Gomera

Island in fact. Captain Khalil was intrigued by the report. He believed you might be interested in questioning those people because of your past interest in the Berber people, to whom the Guanches are related. According to the Malian Navy officer who prepared the report, the Guanches are striking in their appearance—very tall, reddish-tan skin, blonde hair and light-colored eyes."

I was speechless and had to sit down for a moment. Then I told Keita that I would be very interested in meeting them, but didn't know how I would get there.

Keita smiled. "Well, I suspected you might show some interest, so I am prepared to lend you one of the two caravels that have accompanied mine here. They are stocked with building material and other supplies. We will unload the cargo of one of them here. The other will be continuing on to our community in Quonambec. I will put the empty caravel at your disposal."

Again, I was speechless for a moment. Then I accepted the offer. "I was preparing to pay a visit to our colleagues in Quonambec, but meeting those Guanches is an opportunity I cannot miss. I propose, then, that you lend me that caravel and its crew for a voyage to Gomera Island. I would of course need to have all identifying markings on the caravel removed."

Keita looked puzzled. "But Nicolas, why go on such a long voyage to a tiny island? Surely there is more to this story than merely a chance to talk to some Guanche people."

With a twinkle in my eye, I chuckled and replied, "There is indeed more to the story. I have been hoping for an opportunity such as this to land at my feet. My dear Duke, do you remember any of the stories I related to you when I first arrived on Santiago Island?"

He scratched his chin and frowned. "Frankly, Nicolas, I have had more important things to think about than your stories from many years ago. Don't make me guess, just tell me what's on your mind."

"Here's what's on my mind, then. Surely you have heard of the notorious history of Admiral Cristoforo Colombo. Yes? Good, I see you are nodding your head. Colombo is an experienced navigator and ship captain from Genoa. He has long been trying to get the Spanish monarchs to sponsor a fleet of ships to sail west. The imbecile, like all the imbeciles on that continent, believes that if he sails west for a few weeks across the Great Ocean, he will each India! Can you believe it??? Those fools have no idea how large our world is, or what lies on the western side of the Great Ocean."

I could see that Keita was interested in what I was about to say. "Of course, we are all hoping that the Malian Navy will continue to successfully block Spanish and Portuguese ships from leaving their ports, and that Colombo will never be able to make his historic voyage of 'discovery' and exploitation. But there is no guarantee of our continued success.

"However, if his fleet does in fact manage to escape our attempts at bottling up those ships in their harbor, we know from the historical record that his little fleet of three ships will be forced to lay over for a little while on Gomera Island for repairs. That's where I hope to arrange to meet the Great Admiral."

Keita looked surprised. "To meet him? You want to meet him, the notorious butcher of the New World?"

I laughed. "Yes, I do in fact want to meet the 'notorious butcher of the New World,' as you so nicely described him! Here's why. My plan would be to have my caravel tied up at the dock on Gomera Island when Colombo's ships arrive. I would already have recruited 15 or 20 crewmembers made up of Guanche people to replace the Malian crewmembers, who will journey to one of the other Canaries to assist in development projects there. I would introduce myself to the Great Admiral as a navigator from Paris and explain that I had planned to cross the Great Ocean in search of trade with India. I would tell him that I was hesitant to make that voyage alone, that I would prefer to sail in the company of other ships. I don't believe Colombo would object. I'm fairly certain that Colombo would welcome another ship's company on that voyage, especially a ship captained by a light-skinned man from Paris and a light-skinned, blue-eyed, blonde crew."

Keita looked skeptical. "But I still don't understand why you would want to accompany Colombo's fleet."

I kept my impatience in check. "Let me explain in more detail. Captain Janaina's report, which you and I have studied, describes her plan. A few days before Colombo's fleet arrives, she and Captains Iracema and Sofia plan to hide the six caravels and pirogues in the southernmost of the two bays that face the Great Ocean. Janaina says that bay is perfectly shaped to allow that. It has a sharp turn to the left as you enter it, making it possible to hide their ships from view. She plans to place a floating barrier, a raft made to look like a small island covered with brush, across the mouth of that bay in order to discourage Colombo's ships from attempting to enter that bay. Instead, his ships will enter the northernmost bay that opens out onto the Great Ocean.

"Once those ships are inside, the captains anticipate that Colombo's crews would disembark and begin exploring the island and meeting the indigenous people. The people would invite the crews to a feast in the large meeting house far from the beach. All 90 Guanahani sailors would be armed and waiting in the hidden bay in pirogues and other small craft. They will move the raft aside and row out from their hiding place. Some of them will climb Colombo's ships' rope ladders and take possession of the ships. The others will pull their boats up onto the beach, ready to meet Colombo and his sailors when they return from the feast. Of course, Iracema, Janaina and Sofia will have had no way of knowing my plan. My ship full of Guanche sailors will wait outside the entrance to both bays until they determine that the Spaniards have left their ships. My crew will assist in subduing Colombo's men."

I paused for a few moments to allow Keita to digest what he had just heard. Then Keita said to me, "I seem to remember you telling me in the past that Colombo had a crew of over 80 seamen. Are you suggesting those men will simply surrender without a fight?"

I laughed and said, "I am indeed suggesting that! They will have left their ships unattended while they are attempting to ingratiate themselves with the local people. Most or all of them will be drunk and drowsy from a full meal. They will be confronted by dozens of armed sailors. The reports don't go any further than that."

Colombo's rude reception

I am proud to say that the Malians' plan worked perfectly. I learned all about the outcome after my own ship full of Guanche sailors arrived and dropped anchor in the large bay. After I had gone ashore, I was greeted by Captain Sofia and two of the local leaders, Siba and Hiriko. When I asked how Colombo's sailors had ended up lying face down on the sand, Hiriko said, "We treated them to a grand feast with plenty of food and drink. Are we to blame if they drank too much and began running this way and that?"

I laughed, but at that moment Colombo himself raised his head from the sand and said to me, "You, Flamel! What's going on here? Do you know these people? If so, order them to release me and my men!"

I smiled and shook my head. "I'm afraid I do not know them, except for this beautiful African lady here. Allow me to introduce you. This is Captain Sofia Amina of the Quonambec-Mali Federation, formerly of Oporto and before that, the headwaters of the Gambia River." I then turned to Sofia and said in French, "This angry and somewhat inebriated sailor is Admiral Cristoforo Colombo, sailing under the flag of Spain. The rest of these sailors on the ground are his crew." I looked around and added, "My goodness! Whatever happened to them?"

Sofia sighed and said, "I'm sorry, Nicolas, but my French is poor. My Portuguese is much better. May I answer you in Portuguese?"

Colombo shouted, "Speak French!"

Sofia laughed and said to me, "Okay. Here's what happened to poor Admiral Colombo and his sailors. We prepared a party for 80 after we learned they were probably going to arrive today. Luckily, we had just enough food and beer on hand. But our guests drank too much and proved to be somewhat rude. They refused to acknowledge our hospitality. They insisted on trying to reboard their ships, those that you see in the bay, but were too drunk. My sailors kept them from charging into the water in that state, for fear they would drown."

Colombo shouted again, "Liar! This is a trap, although I do not know why. Let us end this. Release me and my men."

I said, "You are right, Admiral. This trap was prepared for you. I am afraid I deceived you back in the Canaries. You are now guests of the Quonambec-Mali Federation. You will not be mistreated unless you refuse to cooperate."

"Cooperate!! Guests? Is this how you treat guests, tying their hands behind their backs face down in the dirt? Explain yourselves!"

I complied with Colombo's request. "Well, you and your rulers, Ferdinand and Isabela, would have planned to exploit and enslave the peoples of the New World once they learned it was not India. Myself, Captain Sofia and all the other people you see on this shore, were prepared for your arrival and were determined to put a stop to the aggressions of the Spanish and Portuguese. Consider yourselves our guests. As I said, you will not be mistreated if you cooperate."

Our first order of business was to decide what to do with the Admiral and his crew. For the rest of the afternoon and evening, they were separated from one another. The Guanche sailors moved them to several warehouses used for storing agricultural produce and dried fish. Ayoze, my First Mate, spoke fluent Spanish and explained the situation to Colombo and his men. "We cannot release you yet. As a group, you are dangerous. Singly, or in twos or threes, perhaps you would be safe to release. But not here, not on this island. It is already overpopulated and lacks sufficient resources for you."

Colombo frowned. "What do you mean resources? Why don't you return us to our ships? We will return without troubling you further." Ayoze replied, "I'm afraid we cannot do that. We know your history well. We intend to change that history. Master Flamel will explain everything tomorrow morning. For the rest of the evening, get some rest."

Two days later Ayoze and I visited the warehouse where the sailors were housed. We met with Siba and Hiriko and learned that they were organizing a Taino language immersion course for the sailors. Siba laughed as she described Colombo's reaction when he learned he and the sailors would be required to learn what he characterized as a "heathen" language.

I saw Colombo standing near a screened window as if he was trying to breathe fresh air untainted by the odor of drying fish. When he saw me, he walked over and demanded, "Explain yourselves! What are your plans for us?"

I gave the admiral an explanation. "Colombo, there are many fertile islands within a day's sail from here. Many of them have small populations of Taino-speaking people who are subsistence farmers and fisher folk. We have decided to 'distribute' the Spanish sailors throughout those islands, since many of you were farmers and fishermen before you joined this expedition. Who knows, perhaps you and the local people will become friendly, and you may find wives!"

After the language classes began and the sailors became occupied in learning Taino, the Malian sailors and I began inventorying the cargo on board the three ships in Colombo's fleet. We were pleased to find great quantities of things that would be useful to the farming and fishing communities in Guanahani—fabrics, cotton, wool, leather, finished clothing, tools, rope, glassware and lumber of various lengths and types. As I examined the crew roster, I saw that there were several surgeons and carpenters. I told Janaina, "Perhaps you should utilize their skills here on this island for the time being."

After a week I called a meeting of my Guanche crew. I said, "Soon those ships will depart with the Spaniards. At that point, you and I have a choice. We can either return to the Canaries, or we can proceed on a year-long voyage to Quonambec itself."

A lengthy discussion ensued. Most of the men seemed eager to travel to a new land and experience in Quonambec. I said, "If you decide on that voyage, you will need to learn a little Arabic. I will ask one of the local people here who have learned the language to organize a class for you. Siba, for example, has an excellent knowledge of the language, and she visited Quonambec once before with Janaina's crew. Once you feel comfortable with the language, you may depart for Quonambec on one of the caravels traveling there." Several of the men who did not want to proceed to Quonambec voted to remain with the Guanahanis to assist with relocating the Spaniards.

I stayed in Guanahani for two more years before sailing to Quonambec with a crew of Guanche men who had decided to prepare for an attack on a Spanish port in the near future. I decided to remain in Quonambec for another year or two to observe the progress of that land's development.

CHAPTER SEVEN

Back Home!

Finally, in the year 1496, I sailed to my beloved Malian capital, Niumi. I was hoping to settle here for a few years, and was especially looking forward to an extended visit with my old friend Khadijah. When I arrived in January, I was pleased to see her in good health. I asked about her husband Hassan, and she said he had retired from the Navy and was now a harbor master. Their daughters and nephews had joined the Malian Navy and were scheduled to participate in the upcoming attack on the Spanish ports.

She added, "I am worried that there will be casualties in that naval attack, and some of those casualties will be Malian. I fear that the attack will not be as simple as the one I took part in 37 years ago, burning shipping docks and a handful of caravels. No, Nicolas, this expedition has a greatly expanded goal—the complete destruction of the Spanish port of Huelga and all of the ships. There will be fighting, I am sure of it."

I replied, "Khadijah, I wish I could assure you that our forces will be victorious and the power of Spain will be destroyed, utterly destroyed forever. Just like we destroyed the power of Portugal two years ago." Then I chuckled and added, "But, of course, nobody can predict the future."

"Your laughter reassures me, Nicolas. Do you know something that none of the rest of us know?"

"Nothing is certain, my dear. But my vision of the future we are creating reassures me. I was fortunate that my plan came to pass as I had hoped. But let's change the subject. What of your niece, Aliyah, Maryam and Youssef's granddaughter? What news do you hear of her?"

"It has been a few years since she last paid me a visit. She wrote recently to tell me she is very busy in her internship with the Quonambec City government. She's only 16, Nicolas, and I worry she will decide on a career in the Navy, like everyone else in the family."

"Well, I can certainly understand your worry. I have no children myself, but still, I worry about the dangers these young people face today."

"Nicolas, thank you for your concern. Now, about your visit here—what are your plans? Are you going off on a new adventure?"

"No, I am going to remain here in beautiful Niumi for a while. No plans other than that. Except to remove this beautiful amulet that has kept me alive well beyond a normal human lifespan. But I won't remove it quite yet. I want to wait for news of a successful campaign against Spain. And also, I want to work on a project I have in mind."

Khadijah asked, "What's the project you're working on, if I may be so bold?"

I walked to the door, retrieved my satchel, walked back to the divan and sat beside Khadijah. Opening the satchel, I pulled out a sheaf of papers and said, "Here, take a look and tell me what you see."

She took the papers, wrinkled her nose, and said, "Nicolas, these are written in Portuguese. The first page says 'Um Tempo Longe do Tempo.' Nicolas, it's been many years since I've spoken Portuguese,

61 years, in fact. I was a slave in Oporto for five years, which is when I learned Portuguese. The duke who had 'bought' me in Africa—not far from here, in fact—loaned me to a priest when he returned to Oporto. Thanks to that priest, Father Martim Rodrigo, my sisters and I repaired the spherical astrolabe you modified and we came here to carry out your plans. Do these papers tell that story?"

"Only part of the story, my part and those parts played by people I interviewed. I am asking you to supplement the story with the part you, your sisters and Father Rodrigo played."

Khadijah smiled and said, "And the part Gabriel Hugo played."

"Ah yes, of course, my young apprentice back in Paris."

"Well, he was no longer young when Father Rodrigo asked him to repair the astrolabe. Quite ancient, in fact."

No Rest for the Wicked

Six months later, Khadijah and I learned some very good news. The Malian fleet, posing as a Portuguese fleet of some 40 well-armed caravels, destroyed every ship in the Spanish Navy in a pitched battle in the harbor. Then the Malian fleet completely destroyed the entire Port of Huelga. That was the end of the power of Spain forever.

Four years after that, the year 1500, Khadijah and I had a private celebration of the event that changed history—the repair of Father Rodrigo's spherical astrolabe and his sending Khadijah, Sofia and Maryam back in the past to put the world on a better course.

Despite our celebration of the original event that set a new course in the historical timeline, there was still more to be done. I confess I had overlooked another event that I should have remembered—the English naval expedition to the New World across the North Atlantic. I had a plan, but it would require the participation of the priest Father Rodrigo and our mutual friend Gabriel Hugo. So, I composed a letter to Gabriel and had it sent to Oporto via a caravel that was due to depart that morning. Here is what I wrote:

"My dear friend Gabriel. I need you to return to Europe, Paris in particular.

I will meet you there at my home. I have neglected events that will soon occur in England, events that I should have remembered from my previous travels to the future. And the need is urgent.

"*You, my old friend and former apprentice, must convince our good priest Father Rodrigo into joining you! I trust you will believe me when I tell you that this matter is of the utmost importance!*

"*I can only say at this time that the matter concerns the upcoming marriage between Prince Arthur, the heir-apparent of King Henry the Seventh of England, and young Princess Catherine of Aragon. Arthur is in grave danger, although he does not suspect it yet. I alone know of the danger, its cause, and its historic result. Historic, unless we—you and I and Father Rodrigo—can avert the danger.*

"*You no doubt believe it will not be possible to have any influence on those events in England. Do not worry. At this moment, or soon hereafter, Captain John Cabot's English fleet will make landfall in the New World on the island of Guanahani and will encounter Captain Janaina Watu and her officers Ibrahim and Musa of the Malian Federation Navy. Those two officers are the 38-year-old twin sons of Maryam, your former slave in Oporto, and her husband Youssef, one of the freed African slaves. I have sent word to Captain Janaina, asking her to convince Captain Cabot and his fleet to return from the Malian naval base in Guanahani to Paris. Please, please, honor her request. I beg of you! Again, my colleague Janaina will explain everything.*"

I had hoped that those two gentlemen would agree to my request and journey to Paris to confer with me. I was very pleased a year later when my good friend and housemate, Hassan ibn Awolu, announced that Messrs. Rodrigo and Hugo had arrived and were awaiting me in the drawing room of my home in Paris. The date was February 5, 1501. I hugged both of them and said "Welcome to my home."

Father Rodrigo said, "Nicolas Flamel, it is a great honor to finally meet the man I've heard so much about, the man who created that wonderful device that enabled my servants to travel back in time and prevent the diabolical institution of slavery from traveling from West Africa to the New World."

I looked at him and said, "Ah, the good priest I have heard so much about. Your servants did their assigned tasks admirably. Thank you for that compliment, but I assure you it was not I who came up with that plan. It was you! And by the way, I should tell you that your servants Khadijah, Sofia and Maryam, carried out your plan perfectly. Now their legacy lives all around the western hemisphere. And Sofia's grandson Hassan, whom you have just met, has become an accomplished seaman. It was he who piloted the craft that took us here, and who is staying here in Paris for the time being."

Gabriel Hugo looked stunned as he gazed upon me. "My master! How could this be? I recognize you, but it would seem that you haven't aged even a year in the past 83 years! Please explain how it is you haven't aged."

I grasped Gabriel by the shoulders and kissed him on both cheeks. "My dear apprentice! I apologize for leaving you under such sudden circumstances." I paused for a moment and continued, "The spherical astrolabe is the culprit, I believe." I pulled my amulet out from my sweater and said, "This amulet absorbed some of the energy of the astrolabe. It originally belonged to a ninth-century caliph, Haroun al-Rashid of Palestine. It was subsequently acquired in the year 1,000 by Emperor Charlemagne, and I acquired it from him. After I began wearing the amulet while traveling through time with the astrolabe, the amulet must have absorbed the power of the astrolabe. You see the jewel in middle of the amulet? And the fine hair that appears embedded in the jewel? It is said to be a hair from the Virgin Mary. Perhaps that was the source of the amulet's power. The amulet itself eventually became the source of the power to travel through time. It has also stopped me from aging. I found it no longer necessary to use the astrolabe, and left it here.

"But I suspect the amulet's power is waning. It might not work well any longer as a time machine unless used in combination with the astrolabe. However, as I said, the amulet has one other very important power. As long as I wear it, the aging process is kept at bay. Despite my appearance, I am over 160 years old."

My two friends were speechless for a few moments. Then Father Rodrigo asked me, "So, do you know whatever happened to my parishioner Horacio Fuente's astrolabe? It was his that Gabriel and I modified, the one that the sisters Khadijah, Sofia and Maryam used to travel back to Mali in the year 1446."

I replied, "Khadijah told me she had planned to store Fuente's astrolabe in her home in Niumi. She was my companion Hassan's great aunt, sister of his grandmother Sofia. Also stored in Niumi is a large, leather-bound book bearing the title 'Um Tempo Longe do Tempo.' I collaborated on that book with Khadijah. The plan was to present the book to Khadijah's grandniece Aliyah. Khadijah and I wrote it in Portuguese. It tells the complete story of how our alternate history came into being.

"As for my own astrolabe, it is safely stored here in my home. I have a plan for it once all our other plans have been completed." I turned to the priest and said, "You, Father, are instrumental in that plan, but just be patient."

At that point, Hassan announced that our chef, François had prepared our evening meal. During the meal there was much conversation about Hugo and Rodrigo's journey from Portugal to Paris. And that conversation naturally led to their questions about how Hassan and I arrived in Paris from Niumi, which Hassan explained was the capital of the newly created Federation of nations on both sides of the Great Ocean. He told them that the original name was Portuguese—"Mali-Atlantico Federação." I said, "It was a long trip, very long. And at times perilous. Not so much because of the normal risks of ocean travel, but because of the intermittent warfare between France, Spain and England."

Rodrigo interjected, "And Portugal as well? As we departed from Portugal to begin our journey here, we had some concern that we would be attacked by hostile ships."

I shook my head. "No, Hassan and I didn't need to worry about that particular conflict. Our ship was one of those caravels belonging to the Federation. It was well-armed, of course, but our course kept us well away from the coasts of Portugal, Spain and France. It was only when we began our approach to the Channel between France and England that we worried about an attack from either country.

"But at that point, France was engaged in a war in Italy, and England was at peace for the moment. As a result, we were not attacked. Our ship docked at the Port of Honfleur, and Hassan and I traveled to Paris by coach. We arrived not long ago. The other 10 sailors aboard our ship have stayed behind at the Port and are enjoying the French coast."

Rings for the Royals!

After we finished our dessert, François prepared a wonderful drink called "qahwa" that he obtained from our Arab friends. Gabriel was the first to speak. "Monsieur Flamel, your letter indicated you had a specific purpose in asking us to join you here in Paris. What do you have in mind?"

I said, "Well, before we discuss our plans, allow me to show you around the house." I took them upstairs and showed them the upper rooms—a bedroom on each side of the hall and a library at the end of the hall. Then I led them down the back stairs to the salon. I showed them the view of the garden through the window but explained the evening was too chilly for a tour.

Then I got down to business. "You asked about my plans for you. My purpose has to do with the English exploratory expedition to the New World commissioned by King Henry the Seventh."

My comment apparently took their breath away, because they seemed stunned. Rodrigo was the first to speak. "Monsieur Flamel, please enlighten us. We had not heard of such an expedition."

I answered, "Let me tell you what I learned last year before I decided to embark on this journey to France. On one of my trips to the future before my amulet lost its 'charm' so to speak, I learned of some important events in English history, what I would call 'parallel history.' Here is one event I am sure will interest you. The present English monarch, King Henry the Seventh, would die of consumption on April 21, 1509. His successor would be his second-oldest son, Henry." I paused and then continued, "According to the history I studied, Henry's reign as Henry the Eighth ushered in a disastrous period, a cataclysm in fact."

Again, my friends were stunned into silence. Rodrigo said, "I have two questions. First, why wouldn't Prince Arthur become king, since he was the older brother? Second, why was his younger brother's reign disastrous?"

I answered, "Your first question is the most urgent, and the answer to it will render the second question moot. In the history that I studied in my voyage to the future, I learned that soon after Prince Arthur's marriage to Princess Catherine of Spain, he contracted a disease the doctors called a 'sweating sickness' that killed him but spared Catherine. The date of his death in that alternate future was the second of April, 1502. King Henry was then obliged to name the younger brother, Prince Henry, as his successor. As I mentioned, that younger brother became Henry the Eighth and his reign became a disaster for the entire world. We cannot allow that future to come to pass!"

Father Rodrigo asked, "But what could we possibly do to prevent Prince Arthur from contracting that deadly disease? We—Hugo and I—have never even met any members of the English aristocracy."

I arose and gestured to the doorway leading to another room. "Let us go into my laboratory and I will explain my plan to you." The four of us—Gabriel, Rodrigo, Hassan and myself—walked out of the dining room and into my laboratory. Once inside, I turned to everyone and said, "Although none of us has ever met the prince, a man who has met him is on his way here from his aborted voyage to the New World. His name is Captain John Cabot. He was commissioned by King Henry to explore the New World in the hope of establishing trade relations with the rulers of China.

"However, the importance of Captain Cabot's abandonment of his mission is twofold. First, he learned that the land of China lies far beyond the western side of the continent he and the other explorers have called the New World. And second, he alone would be able to arrange our introduction to the prince and his new bride."

Father Rodrigo said, "It sounds like you're saying Captain Cabot already knew the prince. Is that right?"

"Yes, that is correct. He met the prince when the prince was a young adolescent. In fact, the prince is still quite young, as is Princess Catherine."

Gabriel looked about the room, momentarily distracted by what looked like a jeweler's work shop. Then he turned to me and asked, "So, I'm guessing that Cabot's familiarity with the young prince will enable him to obtain an invitation to the wedding. Is that what you're suggesting? But why would Cabot be interested in asking that we— Father Rodrigo and myself—be allowed to attend the wedding?"

"Ah, now we get to the reason we are standing in my laboratory. Maybe you have noticed a tray of small gold bands and a small jar of gemstones on the counter." I turned to Hassan and said, "Would you be so kind as to explain to our guests the nature of the gemstones and where you found them?"

Hassan walked to the counter and removed several of the stones from the jar. He held them out and said, "These are emerald-green chrome tourmalines. Although they're rare, I found these in my home country of Quonambec, southwest across the Atlantic Ocean. A traditional healer there sold me 20 tourmalines, each approximately seven millimeters in diameter. Emerald-green chrome tourmalines have magnetic properties capable of 'untangling'—to use an interesting word—roadblocks in the body's energy passages." He handed two stones to Gabriel and two to Rodrigo, who examined them closely before handing them back. Hassan kept the remaining 18 tourmalines in his hand.

Gabriel turned to me and said, "Monsieur Flamel, what do you plan on doing with the stones?"

I chuckled and said, "What I will do is hand all of them to you. I will ask you to set one stone in each of 20 gold rings, which you will design and make. My little laboratory is equipped with gold solder, jeweler's torches and other tools and materials."

Father Rodrigo smiled. "Ah, I understand your plan. But I am confused. Two of the rings will be presented to Prince Arthur and Princess Catherine on the occasion of their wedding in England. You are counting on the rings to counteract the disease." He paused and continued, "How that would come about, I don't understand. Nor do I understand how you would know their ring sizes.

"But what I also don't understand is why you ask Hugo to make 18 additional rings. Who would those rings be for?"

I answered, "First, let us go to the work bench and I will answer those questions." We walked to the bench and I continued, "The properties of the tourmalines, as I said, include assisting the body's energy flow, through an inherent magnetic property of the stones. That property is well known among indigenous peoples all over the world.

"The illness that Prince Arthur and Princess Catherine would contract—unless prevented by these stones—is similar to a disease common in tropical regions. The indigenous peoples of those regions often wore jewelry made from these stones to combat the fevers and sickness caused by the disease. Other persons who might also contract the disease would be King Henry's youngest daughter, Princess Mary, his other son, Prince Henry Junior, their spouses when they eventually marry, and other people who will receive the rings as gifts."

Gabriel asked, "But how would such a disease occur in a region like England? Surely the disease you speak of is one only found in the tropics."

I shook my head and said, "You may have forgotten that England has had trading relationships with countries in the tropics. It is likely that the diseases traveled to England along with the animals and trade goods obtained in the tropics."

Gabriel said, "And my second question: their ring size? How will I make rings of the correct size?"

"The two rings for Henry Junior and his eventual betrothed will be sized for a child's hand. You only need to approximate their sizes. A jeweler can adjust them as necessary. And the other rings' sizes can be altered later as necessary."

Gabriel asked one more question, "You spoke of Mary's and Henry Junior's spouses 'when they eventually marry.' Do you know something we don't know?" When Gabriel asked this, he smiled knowingly.

"Of course, I know something you don't know! You should have no doubt by now. Those two will marry, without a doubt. I am working on my plan as we speak."

I watched as Gabriel began working at the jeweler's bench. After two hours, he had finished setting a stone in a gold ring and showed it to me. I told him it was beautiful and urged him to continue working on the other rings. I then explained that Hassan and I had to depart on other business.

CHAPTER EIGHT

The First Meeting with King Henry

It was November 25, 1501, when I next saw Gabriel and the priest. My ship, a caravel that I had painted a dark blue to blend in with the dark ocean, docked at Bristol Harbor at the same time as a Federation ship captained by Janaina Watu. As we greeted one another, we noticed Captain Cabot, his wife Mattea Jacobella, and their three sons Sebastian, Lewis and Sancio. After introductions, Mattea told me that I had just missed the royal wedding of Prince Arthur and Princess Catherine, which had taken place 10 days before. The royal couple were now residing at the royal residence at Ludlow Castle in Shropshire.

As we talked, who should I see approaching but Father Rodrigo and Gabriel Hugo! More greetings and conversation ensued. Hugo told me about the Cabots' voyage across the Atlantic and their arrival at Bristol on November 8th. He told me about two other passengers—a Norse man named Balder and an Onondaga woman named Aponi. Both of them had joined the crews when the ships had spent some months assisting the Beothuk people on one of the islands in the New World. I looked forward to meeting them.

Father Rodrigo informed me that he and Hugo had presented the rings to Prince Arthur and Princess Catherine at a luncheon with the king. They were pleased and put them on immediately. They said they would wear them always. I also learned that at the luncheon, the Cabots described their voyage to the New World, their encounters with the Beothuk people and the people of the Guanahani Islands. When Mattea informed the king that Admiral Colombo's fleet had reached Guanahani and settled there, he was astounded. Mattea then introduced Balder and Aponi, who described how they ended up joining the Cabot expedition. They gave a full account of their encounter with Captain Janaina Watu, who described the origin of the Federation.

It was Father Rodrigo and Gabriel Hugo who answered Princess Catherine's question about the past hostilities between Spain and Portugal. She said, "Aponi, Lady Jacobella and Captain Cabot, I presume you are aware of the history of hostilities between Spain and Portugal in the recent past. Have you come to any conclusions as to the reasons for those hostilities? My family, and all the royals and people of Spain, are deeply concerned by those hostilities, in particular the reason for them. As far as anyone can discern, Portugal and Spain had not been enemies before the hostilities began. To what do you attribute those hostilities? They have created much hardship, and both countries have suffered tremendous economic losses, especially to our shipping industries."

Father Rodrigo told me that after Captain Cabot replied that he knew nothing of the hostilities, he asked Rodrigo if he would care to reply to the princess's question. Rodrigo explained to her that he believed that "the hostilities were related to Portugal's repeated and pervasive attempts to create an economy based on slavery, in particular the enslavement of Africans." The priest then elaborated that his theory was that "some of Portugal's wealthy shipowners and other members of the mercantile class seized on that idea in order to compete more effectively with Spain." Then Hugo added that the ensuing battles between Spain and Portugal over their attempts to expand the slave trade ended up convincing the mercantile classes of the two countries that hoping to profit from the slave trade was a hopeless endeavor. In Hugo's opinion, the attacks had become a thing of the past. I was relieved to hear those accounts of the luncheon with the king on November 8th.

Now I learned that there would another luncheon with the king tomorrow, November 26th. As I was contemplating that luncheon, Captain Janaina said to Mattea, "Madame, when last we met you asked whether Admiral Cristobal Colombo had survived the Atlantic crossing. Well, indeed he did survive. More than survive—he and his crew now work for the Federation. When he learned of our plan to sail across the Atlantic to meet the royal family, he asked to join us. He, his wife and two children are on board as we speak. They will join us tomorrow at the king's reception in the Customs House."

The Customs House's large, open inspection area had been transformed into a grand reception room. Carpets had been laid out, and tables of different sizes and shapes had been set out around the room. On one long table serving people had begun setting out an array of hot dishes. The King had not arrived yet but his staff informed us that he should arrive in less than an hour.

Admiral Colombo's wife, Caoma, was sitting at a round table near the front of the room with Captain Janaina, Mattea, John, Sebastian, Aponi and Balder. Colombo's chair next to Caoma was empty. Caoma had the appearance of a native of the New World, with bronze-colored skin, black hair and eyes, and a slender frame. She and Janaina were talking about something amusing with Balder and Aponi. John and Sebastian listened intently.

Seated at a square table on the left side of the room were Sebastian's younger brothers, 17-year-old Lewis and 15-year-old Sancio, and Colombo's two daughters, Malulani and Surey. The daughters appeared to be 10 or 11 years old and strongly resembled their mother. They seemed to be enjoying talking to Lewis and Sancio.

I was seated at a square table on the right side of the room with Hassan, Rodrigo and Hugo. Hassan was doing most of the talking. I was distracted and kept looking at the king's table. That table was long and rectangular and was positioned at the head of the room just inside the door. Its six chairs sat empty.

After we had finished eating almost an hour later, the king came in. He was accompanied by his wife, Queen Elizabeth of York, their 6-year-old daughter Princess Mary, their 10-year-old son Prince Henry, Admiral Colombo of the Federation and Admiral Reginald Bray of the English Navy.

The king smiled and said, "Good day to my honored guests. I apologize for being late. If everyone has enjoyed their luncheon, I shall begin by explaining why I have invited you all to this gathering. You have all met Admiral Colombo of the Malian-Quonambec Federation on my left. I would first like to say how much I appreciate and value the briefings I have received from everyone at this gathering, especially Captain Janaina. Admiral Bray will now summarize his understanding of the political situation on both sides of the Atlantic."

The admiral stood and smiled at everyone, especially Captain Janaina. Then he spoke. "I had a most interesting discussion with Captain Janaina and Admiral Colombo. Perhaps 'interesting' is too mild a word. 'Astonishing' would better convey my reaction upon hearing what they had to say.

"First and foremost was learning of the existence of what those two leaders of the Federation created under the name of the Mali-Atlantico Federação. Why was the name originally in Portuguese, you may wonder? Well, it turns out that the founders of that federation were Portuguese-speaking people from Mali and Portugal. Two of our guests today—Father Rodrigo and Monsieur Nicolas Flamel—will perhaps explain that connection at another time.

"But the most important fact, at least to me, a military man in command of a modest navy, was what was proposed at our meeting—a proposal that was most enthusiastically agreed to by our monarch and myself. Ladies and gentlemen, England as of today is now a proud associate of this Federation, which seeks to ensure the peace and prosperity of the countries on both sides of the ocean. Our two navies will go far towards meeting that goal!

"England's navy consists of some 14 ships—the Sweepstakes, the Mary Fortune, the Grace à Dieu, the Governor, the Martin Garcia, the Mary of the Tower, the Trinity, the Falcon, the Bonaventure, the Caravel of Eu, the King's Bark, the Margaret, the Regent, and the Sovereign. The Federation's navy consists of over70 ships, almost all of them fast-sailing, maneuverable caravels.

"Now, of course, England is at peace with everyone—or should I say almost everyone. The Royal Family is now well situated with respect to Spain with the marriage of our Prince Arthur and Aragon's Princess Catherine. Our relations with Portugal are excellent thanks to the work of Father Rodrigo here. Our relations with the Dutch, Germans and Italians are peaceful. We hope to expand our relations with the Queendom of Navarre.

"It is only with the French that we have had any worries. Presently we are at peace. But that hasn't always been true, as we all know. Since the turn of this century, France has been engaged in the Hapsburg-Valois Wars for the takeover of several Italian city states. We do not know if those wars will continue, or what adventures France will embark on after the Italian wars end.

"King Henry has come up with a brilliant plan to keep France from becoming our enemy once again. I am not at liberty to discuss that plan at present. In any event, it is still merely a plan. Perhaps it will come to fruition; we shall see."

Admiral Bray paused when the king signaled that it was time that the meeting be concluded. The king announced, "Friends and esteemed guests, there are many important matters to be discussed later today. I sincerely hope we will have some exciting news to announce in two days' time! For now, let us enjoy what's left of this glorious autumn before Old Man Winter announces his arrival!"

We Create a Delegation to the Europeans

On the following December 3ʳᵈ, Janaina, Aponi and I arrived at Ludlow Castle to continue our discussion of our plan to create a royal English/Malian delegation to approach certain leaders of Europe and urge them to join the proposed "Malian-Atlantic Federation." Queen Isabella was present at the meeting. The European leaders and the delegation would discuss how best to counteract imperialistic and destructive monarchial movements wherever they threaten the peace, for example the movements in central and eastern Europe—primarily Germany, Austria, Italy and Russia.

One of the first things that occurred when we arrived for the meeting was that we learned that Isabella had been applying mercury to her skin as a treatment for insect bites. Janaina informed her of my research into mercury, that it was a dangerous poison when applied to the skin. The queen was surprised to hear this, but agreed to cease using mercury on her skin. Janaina reminded her of the disease-preventative powers of Gabriel Hugo's rings, and the queen agreed that she and her husband would be more vigilant in wearing the rings at all times.

By the end of that week, on December 10ᵗʰ, our group had decided to send representatives to Queen Anne of Brittany; Muhammad the Twelfth, Emir of Granada, commonly known as "Boabdil;" and the parents of Anne of Navarre. The goal would be to encourage them to unite in the newly created Federation. King Henry explained the plan to those assembled at Ludlow Castle. "Prince Arthur has managed to get my wife Queen Elizabeth of York to agree to take our younger son Prince Henry Junior to Navarre to conclude the ongoing negotiations with Anne's parents, King John of Navarre and Queen Catherine of Navarre. The negotiations concern the proposed marriage of our 10-year-old son Henry to their 10-year-old daughter Princess Anne. Arthur's mother-in-law, Queen Isabella, has agreed to accompany them in order to discuss the importance of Navarre joining the Federation. As she told me yesterday with a smile, 'I'm fairly certain that those who control Navarre will be most relieved to learn that Spain no longer has any plans to absorb them.'"

The king continued, "At the same time, John, Mattea, Father Rodrigo, Hugo and Janaina will travel to Brittany and meet with Queen Anne of Brittany. Her residence is the Château du Clós Luce. They will urge her to join the Federation in order to counteract the power of her husband, King Louis who ceaselessly strives to stifle Anne's efforts to maintain Brittany's independence from France. We hope that Anne will be particularly receptive to the proposal presented to her, especially when Captain Janaina describes the Federation's origin and current status.

"Here is what we propose: In order to prevent the absorption of Brittany into France, the Federation would assist Anne in keeping Louis from completing that absorption. The Federation would do this by preventing Anne's 'historical' death from a kidney stone attack on January 9th, 1514. In order to achieve that, the envoys would convince her to constantly wear one of the emerald-green chrome tourmaline rings crafted by Gabriel Hugo.

"I will remind you all of the information provided to us by Monsieur Flamel that in what he calls the 'alternate future,' Anne would fall ill and die of a kidney stone attack. The ring crafted by Gabriel Hugo contains one of the powerful stones obtained by Flamel's colleague, Captain Hassan of Mali. That stone is known in Quonambec and throughout the New World to have great healing powers. Queen Isabella has already received two of Hugo's rings for the same reason and she and King Ferdinand have begun wearing them.

"Anne of Brittany is well-known advocate of preserving her country's independence. She is no longer a child, but a Dowager

Queen, and determined to ensure the recognition of her rights as sovereign Duchess from that point forward. Although Louis exercises the ruler's powers in Brittany, he formally recognizes his wife's right to the title 'Duchess of Brittany' and issues decisions in her name. Anne has personally retained rights to the duchy, and the couple's second child, whether son or daughter, would be Anne's own heir, thus keeping the duchy separate from the throne of France. If the emerald-green chrome tourmaline ring she wears prevents her untimely demise, she will remain de facto Queen of Brittany far longer than her husband Louis will remain king."

The king paused, took a sip of water, and then breathed deeply before continuing. "Now, moving on. Nicolas, Hassan, Colombo and Aponi—you all have a very difficult, yet interesting, task. You will travel to Granada to convince the powerful Muslim Emir Boabdil of the wisdom of joining the Federation. Captain Hassan is included in the delegation because of the added influence of a fellow Muslim— especially a Muslim with the powerful rank of Captain in the Malian Federation's Navy.

"Colombo's presence in that delegation will no doubt astonish and please the Emir Boabdil, who had believed that Spain's Admiral Colombo had been lost in the Atlantic Ocean, but has now become an emissary of peace from Queen Isabella and King Ferdinand.

"Finally, the presence of Aponi, an Onondaga woman from a different region of the New World from Captain Janaina, who is from Quonambec like Hassan. Aponi will further reinforce Boabdil's confidence in the Federation's peaceful motives, since she represents those of the far north of the New World, very far from Quonambec.

"I think I have adequately set out the parameters of your tasks. The substance of your negotiations you already know—Janaina had earlier negotiated with Prince Arthur concerning the precise relationships the parties envision between Europe and the Federation. Each delegation will present those ideas to their receptive recipients."

Meeting with Queen Anne of Brittany

Although I was not to be in the delegation to Queen Anne of Brittany in February 1502, I received the report of its success from Father Rodrigo as my expedition to Granada was preparing to leave two months later. "Nicolas, we were shocked at the beauty of the Queen's residence in Morlaix, but even more shocked by the beauty of the Queen herself. She was but 25 years old and stunning! She asked us many questions, but the very first question was one we had expected—the fate of Admiral Colombo's expedition across the Atlantic in search of China.

"Captain Janaina introduced herself as a member of the Federation and briefly described it. Then she informed the queen of the nature of the New World, the founding of Quonambec, and the fate of Colombo's expedition. She told the queen of the union of England's navy with that of the Federation.

"Queen Anne expressed her surprise and delight at hearing of the successful attacks on the Portuguese and Spanish ports. She was particularly pleased to hear of the Spanish monarchs' decision to join the Federation and the monarchs' decision to end the persecution of Jews.

"But when we informed the queen of our proposed invitation to Granada, she was shocked. She said she was pleased to hear that Isabella and Ferdinand were no longer seeking to rid Spain of the Muslims. But, Nicolas, when we told Anne that one of our delegates to Granada—Hassan ibn Awolu of Quonambec—was Muslim, she was speechless.

"Lunch was served at that point. As we dined, I brought up the subject of the ring we had crafted for her. I explained that the stone in the ring was reputed to emanate a subtle energy capable of warding off some diseases. When Gabriel showed it to her, she exclaimed at its beauty and asked about the stone. He told her that Hassan had obtained a quantity of the stones from his sources in Quonambec.

Gabriel explained that he had set them in gold rings to present to the royals in our membership.

"The queen asked more questions about the military nature of the Federation and we assured her that our objective was to protect the people of the New World, not to make war on the countries of Europe. She was particularly interested in the trade possibilities with the islands of Guanahani. The meeting came to an end afterwards, and our delegation returned to Bristol."

Meeting the Boabdil!

A few days after receiving the reports from Gabriel and Rodrigo, my particular part in the king's scheme began. The voyage from Bristol to Spain was relatively uneventful. Myself and my fellow "conspirators"—Hassan, Colombo and Aponi—traveled in my caravel. We approached the southern coast of Spain on April 15, 1502. I called a meeting before we docked and reminded everyone of our task. "We will be presenting our proposal to Muhammad the Twelfth, Emir of Granada. He is 42 years old and is known as Boabdil. He is the twenty-second ruler of the Emirate of Granada. He should remember that we are coming because Queen Isabella sent a message to him as soon as King Henry presented his plan to our group.

"Hassan, we will be counting on you to make a good impression on him as a fellow Muslim when you introduce us. You might point out that many of the original founders of the Federation were Muslims from Africa.

"And you should also point out two important facts. First, the King of England has pledged to eliminate prejudice towards Jews in England. And second, one of our members in the Federation is a Jewish woman from Venezia, Italy: Mattea Jacobella.

"The reason I mention these two facts is that the only non-Muslim population of any significance within the Emirate are Jews, who are generally concentrated in certain cities. Among them are long-established families who have lived here for generations as well as recent arrivals from the Christian north. Of the latter, some had fled during the Christian advance in the 13ᵗʰ century, fearing political change, while others fled later during persecutions under the newly established Christian kingdom.

"The largest Jewish community is in Granada. The Jewish population within the Emirate has been estimated at around 3,000. As of ten years ago, 110 Jewish households were counted in Granada. Jews are prominent in professions such as merchants, interpreters or translators, doctors and professors.

"Boabdil granted Jews a protected status called 'dhimmi' that gave them legal rights to their religion and a certain legal autonomy for their community. We certainly want to reinforce his decision."

I paused and turned to Colombo and Aponi. "You will talk about the discovery of the New World. The European discovery, that is. Others discovered it thousands of years ago, crossing to the New World from the continent to its west that includes China. The New World was well populated before the Spanish fleet arrived in Guanahani. You should emphasize the inclusive nature of the Federation, pointing out that you, Colombo, are married to a native woman and have children with her.

"Aponi, you as well might speak of its diversity, as you are an Onondaga woman from a group of people who live in the far north of the New World who have developed a sophisticated civilization. You could describe your meeting with the three leaders of the Haudenosaunee Confederacy in that land, Tekahawíta, Jikonhassee and Ayenwatha."

Late the next morning, our caravel docked, the crew stayed with the ship, and the four of us emissaries walked up the hill to the Emir's castle. We were granted entrance when we arrived and soon met the Emir. I was shocked at his appearance—he was short and looked bent and shaky. He noticed my shock and explained, "Yes, I am not the man I used to be. I'm afraid that although my kingdom is no longer at war with the combined Castille-Aragon Kingdom, the battles they waged against Granada have afflicted our people considerably, especially me."

The Emir motioned to seats across from his desk and told us to sit down and be comfortable. He then said, "Isabella's message also informed me of the substance of your visit. You wish to invite Granada to join your so-called Federation, is that right?"

I said, "That is correct. Let me introduce the members of our delegation. I am Nicolas Flamel of Paris. To my right is Admiral Cristoforo Colombo of Spain, whose voyage to the New World did not reach China but was a success in other ways. Next to the Admiral is one of the inhabitants of the New World, Aponi, an Onondaga woman. And at the end is Hassan ibn Awolu, an officer in the Federation's navy."

The Emir's look of surprise was palpable. "I must say I am overwhelmed by this information. You have introduced a young woman from the New World, the Spanish admiral who was long thought to have been lost at sea, and a Muslim man of African appearance! I must acknowledge the young lady first. Aponi, I am honored to meet someone from the New World."

Turning to Colombo, he said, "Admiral, I am honored by your visit and look forward to learning more about your voyage."

Then, to me, he said, "Monsieur Flamel, I have heard so much about you. Welcome to my kingdom."

And then the Emir turned to Hassan and said, "Salaam alaikum, Hassan! I did not expect to see a fellow Muslim in your delegation. Welcome to Granada!"

The Emir looked a bit breathless, but then recovered and asked Aponi to say something about herself.

She smiled, gathered her thoughts for a moment, and said, "Your Eminence, my people are from a distant land across the western sea. They are the Onondaga people. I was but a girl on one of their boats when a group of our enemies, the Mikmak people, attacked us as we were exploring the strait to the southwest of an island known as Beothuk. I alone was rescued, saved by people from the island and adopted by an elder there named Dogajavik."

The Emir was silent for a moment. Then he nodded and said, "I would like to hear more, but first, Admiral Colombo, tell me about your voyage. Why did you not return to Spain to report on your success?"

Colombo smiled, "Well, Your Eminence, we encountered a great civilization where we landed. The people there welcomed our crew and invited us to join them. That was when we learned of the Federation, which my colleague Hassan will describe."

The Emir turned to Hassan and said, "Tell me about yourself first, please."

Hassan cleared his throat and said, "Your Eminence, mine is a very humble story, although my forebears' stories are noble.

"My full name is Hassan Ali. I am a grandson of Sofia Amina and Hassan Jibril, who had named their son Awolu ibn Jibril in honor of Awolu, one of the African slaves who had been rescued from the docks at Lagos, Portugal when the Malians burned those docks and captured several caravels in 1459. Sofia and Hassan's son Awolu then married and had a son, me, Hassan Ali."

The Emir said, "Ah, so the story I have heard of Malian ships attacking Spain disguised as Portuguese ships is true! Fascinating! I certainly want to hear more about this Malian navy, or is it the so-called Federation navy?"

"The navy is the Federation's. The Federation is an economic and self-defense association composed of Quonambec, Guanahani, Mali and other nations on both sides of the Great Ocean. England, France, Navarre, Brittany and most of Spain are the latest members. We invite Your Eminence to join us on behalf of Al Andaluz and the rest of Spain."

The Emir sat back in his chair and took a deep breath. "You say economic and self-defense. I assume by economic you mean trade and exploration. But tell me more about self-defense. From what or from whom?"

"From decaying monarchies, primarily, Your Eminence. All over Europe royal families are increasingly self-destructive and dangerous to one another. You only have to ponder the history of Spain itself to begin to understand how much more dangerous the situation is becoming in the rest of Europe."

"But what kind of aid can the Kingdom of Granada provide? We have no coastline on the Great Ocean, only the Mediterranean."

Hassan nodded and said, "You can do much with our aid. The Italian states are in a perennial state of war with each other and with other countries. They send armies to the Holy Land and attack the peoples there, Muslims and Jews… and even Christians whom the Italians believe to be Muslims because of the way they dress and because they speak Arabic."

"Yes, I have heard of those organized forays into the Holy Land. Most are instigated by the Church, is what I have heard. They are called 'Crusades.'"

"Certainly, the Church is part of the reason, but the wealthy in Europe also provide material aid to those crusades."

"You say my kingdom can help. How so? We have no navy, and our army was decimated by the Catholic monarchs during their war against us."

"Your Eminence, the Federation possesses a navy of over 70 ships, and as you have noted, our navy has engaged in battles in the past. We can do so again. With your leave, the Federation could deploy a few ships to your port at Malaga. Those ships would remain under the joint command of the Federation and your kingdom. That Malagan Navy could do much to interrupt the attacks of the Italians on the innocent people of the Holy Land."

Hassan's explanation seemed to perk up the Emir. At least for a moment. But then he slumped back in his chair and sighed. "But I fear I have no energy left after the long-running disputes with the Catholics."

I smiled and said, "Your Eminence, perhaps we have a remedy for your lack of energy." I reached into my bag and pulled out a small wooden jewelry box and handed it to the Emir. "Open it, Your Eminence."

The Emir did so and gasped. "Oh, my. A ring. A golden ring with an exotic gem of a type I have never seen! What is it?"

"The stone is an emerald-green chrome tourmaline. My colleague Hassan is from Quonambec, across the Great Ocean. He found a source of these stones and obtained several dozen. Another colleague of ours, Gabriel Hugo, a master jeweler from Paris, fashioned gold rings with these stones. So far, our Federation has presented rings to rulers throughout western Europe."

The Emir slipped the ring onto his finger and exclaimed, "It fits beautifully. But you say it has some sort of healing energy. How so?"

"The natives of Quonambec wear jewelry made from these stones as a way of warding off disease. From what we hear, the stones are indeed very effective. I urge you to wear this ring; perhaps it will restore your energy for your tasks ahead."

A few minutes later, the Emir invited us to a luncheon. We accepted, and were joined by several of the Emir's nobles. During the luncheon, the Emir announced the idea of the kingdom joining the Federation. When he described the proposal, the notables agreed unanimously. Hassan complimented them and said to the Emir, "Your Eminence, I propose to send four or five of our caravels to your harbor to act as a fledgling navy for Granada. You may appoint a commander and other officers as you deem appropriate. I would also recommend you employ shipbuilders to begin building other caravels. We have several shipwrights who could assist."

"That would be wonderful! I accept your offer!"

Meeting Abraham Zacuto

At that point the luncheon came to an end and the other guests began departing. I asked the Emir if he had heard of the famous scholar and mystic named Abraham Zacuto. The Emir looked shocked. "How do you know Dayyan Abraham?"

I have to confess I was surprised to hear the Emir use Zacuto's title. Then I replied, "I have studied his work for many years. I finally met him some 20 years ago in Salamanca." I glanced around the room to make sure everyone else had left and then continued, "Your Eminence, I was trained in Paris as an alchemist. When I heard of an eminent scholar of oceanic navigation in Spain, I traveled there to meet the man who perfected a navigation device called the astrolabe. I wanted to tell him of my modifications of the device, but he was too concerned about the persecutions of Jews in Spain to really sit down and have a discussion with me. I believe he was planning to move to Portugal."

The Emir smiled. "That is a wonderful story, Nicolas. You will be pleased to learn that not only did the brilliant scholar not flee to Portugal, but he moved here, to my kingdom. He is my guest and gives an occasional lecture at the university. He is very old, though, and I worry about his health. He often talks about moving to the Holy Land to be buried in Jerusalem."

I was surprised. I said, "Living here, Eminence? That is the best news I have heard lately! I wonder if I might have an audience with him. I have much to tell him and I am sure he has much to say to me."

The Emir nodded and said, "I think he would enjoy a visit from you. He hasn't had many visitors of late." We rose from the table and the Emir motioned for me to follow him. He escorted me into Zacuto's office at the rear of the castle and introduced me to him. Zacuto appeared to struggle a bit as he attempted to get up from his chair. I motioned for him to remain seated. I said, "Dayyan Abraham,

I don't know if you remember me but I met you at your home in Salamanca."

He peered at me and said, "Ah, I think I do remember you, Monsieur Flamel. I recall you wanted to discuss the astrolabe. Am I correct?"

"You are correct. That was what I wanted to talk to you about. I still would like to discuss my modifications to the astrolabe, if you would like to hear about them."

Zacuto nodded absent mindedly, but then said, "Nicolas, I'm not sure I'd have much to contribute, or even that my questions would be intelligent. I'm quite aged, of course, and my mind is not quite what it was."

"Well, I have a gift for you that might help improve your health and your mind. Have you heard of the rare stone called the emerald-green chrome tourmaline?"

He nodded and said, "Yes, one of my colleagues years ago, a visiting scholar from Palestine, told me that indigenous peoples believe the stone has some sort of healing power. I don't recall the details, though. As I said, my mind seems to be slipping away little by little."

I reached into my pocket and retrieved the little jewel box I carried. I took out the ring and handed it to Zacuto. "Here, try this on. If it fits, you may keep it. You should always wear it. I believe you will gain some benefit from it."

Zacuto was pleased when he saw that the ring fit his finger perfectly. "I am honored, Nicolas. Let us hope the ring will do me some good. Now, what were we talking about just now? Something about what you have been doing? Was it about the astrolabe?"

I could see that detailed discussion of the modifications to the astrolabe would not be beneficial. But I charged ahead in the hope that he would be an attentive audience, a participant even. "Abraham, many years ago, I managed to modify my own spherical astrolabe in such a way that it became not only a device for navigating the oceans, but also for navigating through time. I used it to travel to the distant future and the distant past. I learned much and have used that knowledge in helping in the discovery of the New World and, more importantly, the protection of the New World from the likes of Spain and Portugal."

I could see that Zacuto was trying to follow my narrative, but was having some difficulty. He nodded and said, "Travel through time, you say?… Yes, I think that might be possible with the right modifications to the device. Rare metals and gems, that sort of thing." He paused and added, "Is that what you did? You made it work?" He paused again and then his eyes lit up. He laughed and said, "You found the manuscript? The one written by my professor, Isaac Aboab of Salamanca?" He was getting more excited.

I was astounded. "Yes, Professor Aboab! He's the one who discovered the way those rare metals interacted when assembled in a certain fashion. His manuscript was published in Hebrew. My wife and I obtained a French copy in 1410. From it we were able to perfect out spherical astrolabe. We made a time machine, Abraham! A machine capable of transporting a person throughout time, the future as well as the past. And we have done it, Abraham, we have done it!"

My outburst in the context of what must have been a revelation seemed to have startled Zacuto. He then seemed to slump down in his chair. "Please, Nicolas, I need to think about what you have said. Give me a moment."

I could see that he was not going to be able to keep up with the conversation, so I said, "Abraham, you have been a wonderful host, and I thank God that I was able to have this visit with you. Please, please, wear that ring always. It will help you, believe me when I say it will help you."

Zacuto smiled and said, "Thank you, Nicolas. I shall. And thank you for paying me a visit."

When I returned to the main sitting room, I saw that the Emir was having a lively conversation with Colombo, Hassan and Aponi. "Ah Nicolas, I hope your visit was fruitful. We have been having a wonderful time, sharing stories and making plans to meet again."

"That's wonderful, Eminence. Yes, my visit was fruitful, although I can see that Professor Zacuto tires easily. He speaks of going home to Palestine. Actually, I think such a trip might be helpful."

After a few minutes, we concluded our meeting with the Emir and departed.

CHAPTER NINE

The Emissaries Disband

It was four months later—August 15, 1502—when the king's emissaries assembled back in Bristol and reported on their progress. King Henry was pleased at the outcome of our efforts. "Now we only have to keep a wary eye on the Ottoman Turks and the Italians."

I said, "Well, I don't think we need to worry much longer. The Federation donated a small fleet of armed caravels to Boabdil so he could expand his navy and begin regular patrols of the Mediterranean. We can expect the Ottomans and the Venetians will exhaust each other with their continual maritime attacks. Perhaps they will do our job for us. In any event, we envision sending envoys soon to Constantinople and Venezia to propose an agreement between them and the Federation."

Henry leaned back and smiled. "Yes, that would be wonderful." Then he leaned back and said, "I do hope everyone here would consider this to be an ongoing project. What I mean is that it seems to me to be something requiring regular oversight."

Janaina nodded. "Yes, Highness. For myself and the others in the Federation, that is our expectation."

Mattea and John said they anticipated remaining in England so that they could give their younger sons some sort of "normal" life. They expected Sebastian to stay with the Federation.

Aponi said she and Balder would also stay with the Federation.

Father Rodrigo and Hugo said they would return to Oporto and keep an eye on the royals there.

The king looked at me and asked, "And what about you, Nicolas? What are your plans? Back to Paris?"

"Yes, Highness, I think I need to return to Paris at some point. My home is in need of some work, and my body and mind are in need of some rest. But for now, I think I shall stay in England and do some writing before retiring to my cabin here on the grounds. And after Paris… who knows? I suspect I shall pay a visit to my friends in Niumi. We shall see.

"But before I leave Paris, I have something I need Father Rodrigo to do for me." Turning to the priest, I said, "Father, do you recall me telling you when you and Gabriel were at my home in Paris that I had a special task for you?"

Rodrigo thought for a moment, then said, "Yes, something to do with your spherical astrolabe?"

"That's correct. I have it with me here in Bristol. I am tired of carrying it with me everywhere, a useless piece of baggage is what it has become. After all, it was Horacio Fuente's astrolabe that you and Gabriel modified, not mine. I would like for you to take mine home to the Church in Oporto. Please ask the bishop to accept the astrolabe as a donation to the Church's archives. I feel my astrolabe will be safe there for the time being."

The priest said, "It will be my pleasure. Remind me to put it in my luggage when it is time for me to depart."

I was relieved. I knew from my travels to the future that at the end of the 19th century the Church in Oporto would empty its archives and put everything up for auction. The Church's records of the auction listed my astrolabe as having been bought by a Chinese diplomat named Yi Kang. I read a little about him and learned that he had a reputation as a deeply superstitious man.

In one of my voyages to the future, I located Yi Kang's memoir from the 1960's. Yi Kang wrote that in 1884 while posted in in the Abyssinian city of Harar, he attended an auction and purchased a 400-year-old book bound in black leather. It had Arabic and Amharic characters on the cover, neither of which Yi Kang could read. The text of the book was written in English, another language Yi Kang could not read. I realized the book had been written by Horacio Fuente and stored in a mosque archive in Zeila, Somalia, by his daughter. It was then stolen by the deeply superstitious warlord Ahmad Grañ, who kept it with him in all his battles. Upon Grañ's death in battle, the book ended up in a library in Harar and was subsequently purchased by Yi Kang. In his memoir, Yi Kang frequently stated his belief that the astrolabe and book acted together as some sort of talisman. He wrote that to protect himself he kept them with him always. In 1924, twenty years after his retirement, he bought a very old mansion in Hawaii and lived there for 40 years. In his memoir he mentioned storing the astrolabe and book in the attic.

A New Home for My Spherical Astrolabe

I thought of a brilliant plan. After a few months of rest at my home in Paris, I would travel to Niumi and retrieve Khadijah's astrolabe, the one that Horacio Fuente had modified to become a time machine. I would leave my own book, entitled Um Tempo Longe do Tempo, in Khadijah's apartment, but use the astrolabe to transport me to Hawaii in 1964.

Upon my arrival in Yi Kang's mansion in 1964, I would retrieve my own astrolabe and replace it with Khadijah's astrolabe.

With that plan firmly in my mind, I knew I could take a well-deserved rest in Paris before embarking on my trip to Niumi in a few years.

It was March 21, 1506, when I arrived in Niumi. Khadijah was very ill and slept a great deal. I was worried that she would not live much longer. I was right; she passed away not long after I arrived. Two weeks later I met Khadijah's young grandniece Aliyah, who had come to Niumi to visit her elderly great aunt. Aliyah was shocked and saddened when I informed her that Khadijah had passed away two nights earlier in her sleep.

In an attempt to assuage Aliyah's grief, I handed her my book and said, "Your great aunt, with my collaboration, wrote this in Portuguese, a language that was once an important European language but is now barely read by anyone. Nevertheless, your great aunt knew you had studied the language in your youth. She felt you should read this book to gain a better understanding of the history of your people, the people of Africa and the people of Europe." I paused, then added with a smile, "She also wanted you to learn more of your great aunt's life as well as the lives her two sisters." Aliyah took the book and thanked me.

As she was engrossed in the book, I went into Khadijah's bedroom and retrieved the astrolabe that she and her sisters had modified, the one Father Rodrigo had inherited from Horacio Fuente. I carefully wrapped the astrolabe in a towel and placed it inside my suitcase. Then I walked out into the living room and took leave of Aliyah. "I must leave now. I hope you enjoy the book. Remember what it is—the history of your family and how all this came to be!"

Aliyah said she looked forward to learning more about her history.

I walked out the door, turned left and went around to the rear of the building. Looking around to make sure I was alone, I took out the astrolabe, unwrapped it and set it on the garden wall. I adjusted the first of the two arrows for the geographic coordinates of "Molokai, Hawaii," and the second for the date of "1964." Then I put one hand on the location arrow and my second hand on the date arrow.

As soon as I did that, the scene in front of me blurred, wavered and changed from an African garden to an asphalt road in Hawaii. I hurriedly rewrapped the astrolabe and put it back in my suitcase. I took a look around and began walking down the road towards what looked like a village in the distance.

I passed a sign that read "Kalaupapa." As I drew closer to the outskirts of the village, I saw that the area looked like it was once a grove of palm trees but was now in the beginning stages of a housing development. Several houses were under construction, but there was one magnificent 19th century mansion set back from the road on a cliff overlooking the Pacific Ocean. I guessed that must be the place.

There was a "For Sale" sign posted in front of the mansion. The front door was open and I saw two people leaving. A woman stood just inside the door and smiled as the couple left. I approached, smiled and said, "Hello. I'm relieved to find you still here. You are the real estate agent?"

"Yes. Maryanne Clarke. And you are?"

I shook her hand and said, "Nicolas Flamel. I read the advertisement and thought I'd take a look. My taxi dropped me off at the earlier village by mistake and I've had quite a walk getting here." I paused, set down my bag and said, "Do you mind if I just walk around inside?"

"Sure. I hope you don't mind but some workmen have opened up one of the attics to inspect for roof leaks and that sort of thing. The house hasn't been occupied for a few years and you never know what kind of condition the roof and attics are in. Feel free to take a look in the attic yourself if you like. The ladder is still in place. I'll be in my car finishing up some paperwork if you have any questions."

"Thanks. Don't mind if I do. The house I previously owned had a terrible roof leak and mold in the attic, so I definitely don't want to go through that again."

I walked into the parlor, strolled around a bit, then inspected the kitchen before heading back to one of the drawing rooms. There was a ladder set up under the attic trapdoor. I looked back and didn't see the agent or anyone else, so I climbed the ladder and entered the attic through the trapdoor. As I expected, it was full of junk, including a large crate in the center of the attic. Hoping it was the same crate left in the attic by Yi Kang, I crawled over and opened it. Inside was a steamer trunk full of old clothes. I excitedly pulled out the clothes and found it. "My astrolabe! My beloved astrolabe! After all these years, you are still here!" I took out the astrolabe and set it aside. I opened my bag and unwrapped Khadijah's astrolabe, the one that originally had belonged to Horacio Fuente. I picked up her astrolabe and firmly slammed it against one of the wooden columns holding up the roof, hoping to break the silver wire inside the way Fuente had broken it when he fell all those years before. I lifted up the astrolabe and shook it gently. Hearing a slight rattle inside the little gold globe in the center of the astrolabe, I said, "Yes! The wire is broken! Now it will be up to João da Gama to fix it in the future." I carefully put it in the trunk of old clothes and placed the trunk back inside the crate. I wrapped my own astrolabe in the towel and placed it in my suitcase. Then I crawled back to the trapdoor and climbed back down the ladder.

I walked back outside to the agent's car and said, "Thanks, but this place is a bit too much for me. Not my style, either." I smiled, turned and began walking back up the road to the village. I knew the mansion would change hands several times before eventually being bought by da Gama in 2018. None of the subsequent owners would ever bother to open, let alone inspect, the attics.

As I walked up the road, I asked myself, What now, Monsieur Flamel? Is your work done? I decided to take a room in the village and try to get in contact with Perenelle. "I do hope she has been enjoying herself all this time."

I checked into a room in a charming little inn not far up the road, set down my bag, and walked out onto the little balcony overlooking a beautiful expanse of palm trees. "Ah, this will do very nicely." I turned around, saw the little guest telephone on the nightstand. For a moment I thought I might try to find Perenelle by calling someone, but then I laughed and said to myself *Who would you call? The police?*

CHAPTER TEN

Reunion with My Beloved!

I decided I would return to the future and find Perenelle. The time when we were last together was October 1st, 2018. That date was a few months before da Gama would purchase the mansion. It would be another two months before da Gama would get around to exploring the mansion and discover the trunk in the attic. Finally, a few more months after that, da Gama and his fellow retired professors would be interviewed on a campus radio program to talk about their idea of traveling to Somalia for research. I figured it would be safe to arrive in the future in late mid-December, 2018. By then Perenelle would most likely have gone to Oahu to look for something to do.

Although I actually had no idea where Perenelle might be at that date in the future, I had several ideas. Maybe she will have found employment. She has a university education, she is fluent in German, French and English. Perhaps she will pursue an academic career like she said she might.

I slept fitfully that night, excited yet apprehensive at the enormity of my task ahead—to travel to the future and find my wife! The next morning, I informed the innkeeper that I would be checking out soon. On a hunch I asked him if there were any college campuses nearby. He smiled and said, "No, this island is far too undeveloped. Perhaps in the future. For now, there is only the Mãnoa campus on Oahu." When he said that, I thought to myself, *well, I guess I'll find out.* I paid my bill, and went back to my room. I placed my astrolabe on the desk and set the date for December 15th, 2018. I didn't think it wise to try to meet her at the same time we had parted. I chuckled and said *I certainly wouldn't want to meet myself in the future!*

I decided to "aim" my astrolabe for the University of Hawaii Department of French. I had a hunch that she would try to find work in some capacity in that department, perhaps as an adjunct professor, or at least as an administrative assistant.

I dialed up the location of the French Department, touched both ends of the silver arrow, and I was off to the future! As always, I kind of got a kick out of how the view in front of me changed—my vision wavered, as if I were looking through thick glass. Then I noticed that instead of hotel room furniture, I saw some sort of lounge. Thankfully there was nobody around. Apparently too early for those academic types!

I quickly put my astrolabe in my bag and looked around the room. Some signs were in French and English. But then I was shocked to see some signs in Arabic! And one sign shocked me most of all— "Office of French and African Studies, Quonambec-Hawaii University, Mãnoa Campus." It was directly over a rather grand, double-door entrance to an office. I said to myself, 'Hmm, so the Malians have extended their nation all the way to Hawaii!'

There was a light on inside. I decided to be brave and walk right in. The desk that faced the entrance was grand—large, made of some kind of exotic wood I didn't recognize. A double-screen computer sat on it. Behind the desk was a glass-walled conference room. There were nine or ten people sitting at a long table. A woman sat facing them with her back to me. I wasn't sure, but it sure looked like Perenelle. The other participants were a diverse bunch—Hawaiian,

African, Arab, Hispanic.

I decided to sit at the desk and wait for the meeting to be over. In the meantime, I was trying to figure out what my plan was. Plan? I had no plan other than to rejoin my beloved Perenelle.

Then I had a thought. I recalled that in our "alternate" world—across the so-called interstice between the worlds—a group of University of Hawaii professors would embark on a voyage to the past. I was trying to recall when they would do that—exactly when, that is. I knew how—they would use the spherical astrolabe Perenelle and I had deposited in the attic of the mansion that João would buy.

A date and event came to mind. In about a week, there would be a radio interview on the UH student radio station, KTUH, of the group of retired history professors. The host of the program would be pumping her guests for more information about the groups' plan to visit Somalia. What she didn't know, but I knew, was that the group would attempt to travel back in time, to 1430. The city was Mogadishu, which at that period in history was not yet the battle-scarred hell hole it was today. But who knows, in this alternate world where I was now, perhaps Mogadishu had become a garden. But I doubted it.

So, I figured a good plan would be to try to get hold of João da Gama of the history department, or one of the other professors. I recalled their names: Professor Sandra Bevilacqua taught in the political science department. Professor Abbas Amir taught in the anthropology department. Professors Yuen Ho Wan, Horacio Fuente and Makelle Ringhiera taught in the history department. And Professor João da Gama taught in the history and geography departments.

What I would approach them about was the "$64,000" question, to borrow an expression from some place in time I no longer remembered. I guessed I should probably try to make sure da Gama found and bought the mansion. After all, that's how all this nonsense got started! But I knew that wasn't true—"all this nonsense" got started when I left the modified, but broken, spherical astrolabe in the chest in the mansion. Actually, it began before then, but I don't have time to go into that again.

Speaking of time: as soon as I "decided" what to do, Perenelle came out of the conference room. When she saw me, her eyes opened wide. She smiled but put her fingers to her lips and pointed behind her. The others in the meeting were starting to come out of the room. I stood aside as Perenelle greeted and thanked each of them, in her incomparable French, as they left.

Then it was my turn. She turned back to me, walked over, and gave me a loooong hug. She said, "Dear, we have a lot to talk about, don't we! I think I'll put the 'Out to Lunch' sign on the door, and we can escape to the Dean's Office in the back of the conference room."

I nodded and waited as she put up the sign. Then I followed her as she walked to the office.

She began our "meeting" by describing the series of events that led up to her being there in that gorgeous office with all those exotic people. "Nicolas, I must have been prescient when I told you a few months ago that I would try to get a job in some academic department. Well, I got one but not as a professor. I don't have the academic qualifications—at least not recent qualifications: mine are from a few hundred years ago! How serious would they take me if I tried to present my diploma from that era!

"It was my fluency in French that got me this job as executive secretary to the Department Head."

I interjected, "And who is the Department Head?"

She smiled and said, "You won't believe it, but talk about coincidence—the chief here is none other than João da Gama, who holds a joint professorship in the history and geography departments!"

I was stunned. "That's amazing! And talk about fortuitous. He's the one I was about to talk to you about."

She raised her eyebrows. "Da Gama? Whatever for? Oh, wait.

Something about the mansion, right? Dear, are you planning on setting this whole adventure back in motion? Is that it?"

"That's exactly it. We have a few weeks to talk to da Gama, feel him out, you know what I mean? Find out if he's in the market. I mean, we both remember that with the death of his wife, the departure of his kids for the mainland, and his retirement, he's thinking of 'upsizing' to wild nature. To Molokai, to be exact. And you might remember the name of the realtor who showed him the mansion. Wanna take a guess?

"I don't have to guess. It's Margaret Kahale."

"You have a great memory, my dear! Any idea how we can get hold of her?"

"I think you mean, get hold of João and suggest he get hold of Margaret."

"Well, you're better connected than I am. We both know exactly where the mansion is located, we know who's selling it, and we know a lot about it." I paused and took a breath before continuing. "Perhaps you could do a little 'innocent' inquiring about da Gama's interest in real estate. Tell him you know a fantastic real estate agent, and that you've heard about an old 19th-century mansion on Molokai. I'm fairly certain he'll take the hook. Hell, we both know he'll take the hook!"

"That's a great plan, one that we know will work. So… I'll get on it Monday morning when my boss returns from his retreat with Fuente and Ringhiera. Now that retirement has hit them in the face, they're going all out exploring the islands."

Then she asked me, "I take it you haven't found a place to stay, yet, have you? I just might be able to 'hook you up,' as the kids say, with a room in a classy little apartment in town. Only catch is, you'll have to share a queen bed with the landlady."

"Ooh, that sounds kinda risqué! I accept your offer."

*   *   *

It was December 30, 2018, when we heard back from Margaret. We visited her in her office in Oahu and asked her to fill us in. She smiled and said, "I want to thank you two for hooking me up with this man, da Gama. He was definitely in the market, and he loved the mansion. Although not at first; it had some problems. But I assured him they were minor, and he agreed. He bought it in an all-cash deal. Not only that, but as we speak, he has a crew hard at work replacing windows, roof, carpets, that sort of thing.

"And I enjoyed meeting his fellow faculty members. I learned that da Gama had presented some kind of trip to Africa to them. He told me they seemed skeptical at first but soon agreed to join him. I don't know the details of the trip, but it's related to something they've all studied in their careers."

I nodded and replied, "They're planning on traveling to Mogadishu, is what I've heard."

"Mogadishu? Where's that? And how did you know that?"

Perenelle interjected, "Mogadishu's the capital of Somalia. It's a country in East Africa. I'm the executive secretary in da Gama's university department. He told me about his dream not long after you showed him the place."

Margaret frowned, "But Somalia? Isn't that a war-torn, pocket of desert and poverty?"

I nodded, "Yes, that's true for the most part. But the northern part is actually a peaceful, separate country, Somaliland. Maybe da Gama's group is planning on visiting there."

Perenelle and I knew better. The group was planning on going to Somalia itself, but a few hundred years in the past. It was a virtual paradise in those days, full of every kind of people and the hub of many trade connections with Asia, the Middle East and the rest of East Africa.

As we walked out of Margaret's office, I said, "Well, my dear, do you think you could pull a few strings and get me a job? I'm very tired of traveling back forth all over the world in all its divergent histories!"

She took my arm and said, "I'll see what I can do!"

- - FIN - -

ABOUT THE AUTHOR

After 23 years practicing law with the California Attorney General's Office in San Francisco, and teaching for 13 semesters in Golden Gate's Appellate Advocacy program part time as an adjunct professor, I retired in 2011 and began writing fiction and memoirs. My first opus was a novella, *My Brother's Keeper*, loosely based on the circumstances of my younger brother's murder. Next came a novel, *Stolen Identity*, published in 2015, and its sequel, *Unfinished Business*, in 2017. *Trial and Error*, the third novel in the trilogy that began with *Stolen Identity* came out in 2021. My novel *The Mystic and the Warrior* came out in 2021.

The Starlight Commune is a combination of two previously self-published novels, *The Spherical Astrolabe* and *Around the Horn and Back*.

My short story *One More Race Before We Die* was published in 2019 in the University of Hawaii eZine, Vice-Versa. I included that story in my *Collected Stories* in 2021.

I published three memoirs in 2021: *A Pirate Forever, Life as a Peace Corps Volunteer, Ethiopia and Eritrea, 1972-74*, and *The Happy Wanderer*. While still a law student at Golden Gate, I served on the Law Review and published an article, *"Qualified Immunity for INS Church-Busters? Presbyterian Church (U.S.A.) v. United States*, Golden Gate University Law Review, Ninth Circuit Survey, Volume 20, Number 1, Spring 1990. In the year 2000 I published a memoir of my Peace Corps experience in Asmara, Eritrea, in the Peace Corps Writers anthology, *Eritrea Remembered: Recollections and Photos by Peace Corps Volunteers.*

SELECTED WORK by
MICHAEL BANISTER
(in chronological order)

My Brother's Keeper

A drug courier crashes his plane in a frozen lake in Yosemite's high country. Winston, a Yosemite "valley rat" on the run from killers in his home town, discovers the plane during a winter hike. He off loads the cargo and begins a new life as a drug dealer. After he and his girlfriend are murdered during a drug deal gone south, their two unrelated children, Josh and Kathy, are raised by their respective grandparents. When Josh asks his Uncle Mark for help in finding his "sister," the outcome is anything but predictable.

Stolen Identity

Dushan's dreams had always been unusual—sometimes scary, sometimes exhilarating. But ever since he was seven years old his dreams took on another dimension—it was like he was awake inside them. His mother—who he thought had been killed in the Yugoslavian civil war when he was a baby—was talking to him, telling him she was alive and living with his father—who was supposed to have been lost at sea during a fishing expedition in the North Sea. In each of those dreams, Dushan was unable to respond and tell his parents that he was living with his "adopted" family in California and was best friends with his "stepbrother" Danilo. The two stepbrothers were now teenagers and occasionally popped up in one another's dreams, sharing their impressions after waking up.

However, the time for dreaming was past—they were about to embark on a desperate attempt to escape their abusive father, the man who arranged to steal Dushan from his real father and plant the lie that his real parents were dead. Their attempt succeeded on one level, but the consequences were completely unexpected.

Unfinished Business

The exciting sequel to "Stolen Identity," the story of a stolen boy and his beloved "stepbrother" growing into manhood and bringing their two families together. Now, they discover they have some unfinished business to take care of and some very unpleasant people to deal with. This gripping tale follows these young men and their families through Britain, Ireland and Slovenia as they attempt to put an end to the tragedies that brought them all together in the first place.

Trial and Error

Dushan Sava was in trouble. Accused of stealing the identity of the victim of a horrific traffic accident, and then impersonating him as a college student, Dushan, an illegal immigrant, had to flee the country using the victim's passport. A year later, after having obtained his own passport and returned to the US, he accompanied a friend who would soon join the faculty at Rutgers University. Dushan's former roommate saw him on campus, and Dushan was arrested and put on trial. The outcome of the trial was anything but certain.

The Mystic and the Warrior

Who was the man who called himself Shamsuddin? In post-war Valletta, on the island of Malta, he lived in a part of the city that still hadn't recovered from the destruction of World War Two. In 1955, Shamsuddin lived in a bombed-out post office and sold antiques and other valuable items. When a group of five young men from Istanbul paid a visit looking for such things they had heard Shamsuddin could sell them, the parting gifts he provided them were much more than gifts—the young men soon discovered they couldn't bear to be without them.

Forty years later, Shamsuddin's business had radically changed. He had allied himself with Turgut Evren, a Colonel in the Turkish military. Each man had a hidden agenda—hidden from society and hidden from each other. And the five men who were no longer young? What was their destiny in this evolving story?

Life as a Peace Corps Volunteer Ethiopia and Eritrea, 1972-74

A collection of aerogrammes, memoirs and photos from my two years as a Peace Corps Volunteer in Ethiopia and Eritrea, 1972-74.

A Pirate Forever!

A memoir of my life growing up in Japan, Austria, Germany and California.

The Happy Wanderer

A collection of memoirs of my travel and work, 1974-2021, in Seattle, Tunisia, Berkeley, Turkey, Oakland and Ireland.

Collected Stories

Four stories:

One More Race Before We Die—Three race car drivers killed in a race ask a Las Vegas magician to stage a race to allow the dead drivers to finish the race.

Gino di Lampedusa—A genie on the lam from an evil genie in his own world passes through the veil and asks a Las Vegas magician to help him capture and neutralize the evil genie.

Whitethorn, 1969—a backwoods commune terrorizes a group of back-to-the-land hippies.

My Brother's Keeper—a loosely based story based on the murder of the author's drug-dealing brother.